Sleeping Beauty Dreams Big

Grimmtastic Girls

Grimmtastic Girls

Sleeping Beauty Dreams Big

Joan Holub & Suzanne Williams

Scholastic Inc.

ISBN 978-0-545-78393-4

12 11 10 9 8 7 6 5 4 3 2   15 16 17 18 19 20/0

Printed in the U.S.A.   40
First printing, February 2015
Designed by Yaffa Jaskoll

For our grimmazing readers:

Maddy W., Aijay W., Jolee S., Jenna S., Sarah S., Megan D.,
Sabrina E., Sophia E., Jaden B., Taelyne C., Christine D-H.,
Khanya S., McKay O., Reese O., Andrade Family, Isabella K.,
Eden O., Sofía G., Alexis M., Emily M., Hayley M., Jasmine R.,
Abby H., Reilly H., Ashley H., Tessa M., Riya F., Lana W.,
Micci S., Sophia O., Anh H., Thu H., Collection H., Hailey A.,
Lan Anh H., Rachel B., Caitlin R., Hannah R., Raven G.,
Vivian Z., and you!

— JH and SW

Contents

It is written upon the wall of the Grimmstone Library:

Something E.V.I.L. this way comes.
To protect all that is born of fairy-tale, folk-tale, and nursery-
rhyme magic, we have created the realm of Grimmlandia. In
the center of this realm, we have built two castles on opposite
ends of a Great Hall, which straddles the Once Upon River. And
this haven shall be forever known as Grimm Academy.

~ the brothers Grimm

1

Riding a Unicorn

Rose galloped her white unicorn over hill and dale trying to outrace her worries — and her parents, too. They were no more than half a mile behind her in the family coach.

Her long, glossy brown hair streamed behind her, whipping in the wind. Before they'd all left home that morning, her maidservant had arranged it carefully in curls and waves, all held in place with jeweled clips and fancy sky-blue ribbons that matched the stripes in her blue-and-white dress. One of the jewels was carved with the initials BR, for Briar Rose. Because of a certain Grimm's fairy tale, she was also known as Sleeping Beauty. But she had always preferred to simply go by her middle name, Rose.

She held on tight as she and her unicorn soared over a low stack-stone fence. "Good boy," she murmured when they reached the other side. "Almost there. We'll make it before sunset." A curl blew into her face and she shoved it back. After a long day of riding, her hair was now a wild tangle, and the pins and ribbons all askew.

Up ahead she spotted a magnificent turreted castle, which stood at the heart of the realm of Grimmlandia. All around it were trees, gardens, and rolling hills of lush green lawn dotted with colorful objects, which were still too far away for her to make out clearly.

Slowing, Rose pulled up on a grassy bluff. Equal measures of excitement and trepidation filled her. That castle was Grimm Academy, and it was to be her new school from now on. Her home, too, because it was a boarding school, which meant she would live there.

Her tutors back at the palace had explained that the Academy was really two castles in one. Its middle section was a long, four-story stone building that spanned the sparkling blue Once Upon River like a tall bridge that was connected to Pink Castle on one end and to Gray Castle on the other.

She counted three turrets at the top of each castle. Brightly colored flags flew from poles that extended high from the turrets and also from the outer stone walls.

Leaning forward, Rose lay her cheek along her unicorn's soft, snowy mane. "There it is, Starlight," she murmured to him. "So what do you think of it?"

Her unicorn tossed his head, as if in approval. She'd named him Starlight because at night his horn gleamed almost as bright as a star. He'd been a gift to her from a fairy on the day she was born. Thirteen fairies had attended the party held at her family's palace for her christening that day. Only twelve of them had been invited, though. The thirteenth fairy, angry at being overlooked, had crashed the party and put a curse on her. Which was so *not* her fault!

Yet that had been the start of all of her problems. And it was the reason she'd been sent to this school. Her parents hoped that being here would protect her from that dratted curse. It was supposed to go into effect on her twelfth birthday — just five days from now, on Friday.

She raised her head from Starlight's mane. A shiver swept through her even though the day was warm. Not wanting to think about that curse right now, she started riding for the school.

The closer she got to it, the more details she was able to see clearly. Like that those dots on the lawn were actually *people*. Grimm Academy students, by the look of them. When she drew nearer, her eyes lingered on a group of four interesting-looking girls dead ahead. They stood in a cluster near a beautiful garden, laughing and talking.

Hearing a whoop, her gaze swung toward a bunch of boys on the lawn. They were wearing armor and holding lances, swords, and other weapons. Were they knights? *Ooh! How grimmtastic!* She'd dreamed of becoming one herself many, many times.

As she watched them, one of the boys lifted his sword. After pointing it straight ahead, he made quick jabbing motions with it, pretending to fight an invisible enemy. The other boys looked on, shouting encouragement and advice to him.

"Hey, Starlight. That looks like a jousting team. I wonder if they allow girls in. I bet Mom and Dad would just *love* that, right?" She laughed, but even to her own ears her laughter sounded hollow.

In fact, her parents would be horrified at the very idea of her joining such a team. Lances and swords were definitely on the Danger List. Which was a real, actual, *annoying* list they had made of things she Must Avoid once she turned twelve. Because of that dumb curse.

She carried the list, which her mom had insisted she put in her pocket that morning, with her always. And just about every sharp thing you could think of was on it. Forks, knives, hairpins, ink pens, you name it. And most certainly lances and swords.

Rose barreled onward, not slowing. She was determined to beat the coach carrying her parents and her luggage, and make a grand entrance the whole school would remember! Thinking of that, the daredevil side of her kicked in, and she dropped the reins, letting Starlight speed up as he wished. Knights needed to be able to ride hands-free, so they could hold swords and lances, and even carry people they were saving. She'd practiced this move before and knew it could be dangerous. But it was also thrilling!

When she hit the lawn, the students all heard her approach and turned to stare curiously in her direction. She'd been so busy looking from side to side at her stunning surroundings, however, that she wasn't looking at what was right in front of her.

"Yikes!" she yelled as a boy holding a jousting lance loomed large. At the last minute Rose grabbed the reins and tried to pull up. Too late.

"Hey! Watch it!" yelped the boy, who had wavy dark brown hair. He leaped out of her path just in time.

"Sorry!" she called over her shoulder. Looking back at the boy, she now didn't see the *girl* in her path.

"Eek!" yelled the girl. There was a flurry of pink skirts as the candle-flame-haired girl scrambled to get out of her way.

"Sorry! I'm so sorry!" Rose called to the girl. Finally, she managed to rein in her unicorn. After bringing him to a complete stop, she slid from Starlight's back.

She meant to run over to help the candle-flame-haired girl she'd almost, er, *run over*. However, she paused, seeing that three other girls were already helping her up. Rose noticed that the girl wore a pair of sparkly glass slippers. Interesting.

"You okay, Cinda?" one of the girl's friends asked her. This girl had short black hair and wore a tiara with sparkly blue-green gems.

"No cuts or bruises?" asked another of the friends. This one held a cute nut-brown wicker basket over one arm. She wore a red cape and her long curly hair had red streaks in it.

"I'm fine," said the girl named Cinda. "I was just startled, that's all. No harm done."

"Thank grimmness for that," said the third friend. A goth-looking girl, her dark eyes were lined in black kohl and her lips were glossed a deep red. She wore her blue-streaked black hair in loose, thick braids that were so long they almost touched the grass.

Rose knew that these four girls and all the students on the lawn must be characters from literature. Her own family's origins could be traced to the tales of the Grimm

brothers. And all of the students here were connected with the books of either the Grimms or famous
authors like Andersen, Perrault, Lang, Dulac, Baum, Carroll,
and many more. Still others might even be from nursery
rhymes.

All families in the magical realm of Grimmlandia had
been brought to this land by the famous Grimm brothers,
Jacob and Wilhelm. To keep them safe from something
mysterious and dangerous that lurked on the other side of
a huge wall that surrounded Grimmlandia. And needless to
say, she'd always been curious about exactly what that
could be.

Rose was so busy thinking about this she failed to
notice that her parents had almost caught up with her.
Their coach was rumbling toward the school.

"Look!" said the red-cape girl.

Everyone on the lawn gazed in the direction she was
pointing. Rose hunched her shoulders. She knew exactly
what they'd see. A fancy white coach with silver wheels.
A driver in front and a footman in back, both dressed
in white and silver. Her three leather traveling trunks
strapped on top.

She was supposed to have ridden inside the coach with
her parents. But she'd insisted on riding Starlight instead.
Even though he was a no-no on her parents' Danger List (on

account of his sharp horn), she hadn't been able to bear leaving him behind. She needed at least one friend here.

As the coach pulled to a stop in front of the school, one of her trunks tumbled to the ground. *Rumble! Bumble! Thonk!* It landed on its top corner and sprang open.

"Oh, toadwarts," Rose groaned quietly. It *would* have to be the one trunk that her overprotective parents had packed for her. She watched in dismay as pairs of thick gloves, chain-mail armor, and all kinds of protective gear spilled from the trunk. An iron helmet rolled out, bounced down an incline, and across the lawn. Finally it came to a stop by the jousting boy she'd almost run down only minutes before.

Meanwhile, the two coachmen scrambled down to right the trunk. Rose sprang forward to help.

"No, Princess. You must let us do it," insisted the footman, wagging a finger at her. "Your trunks have pointed corners. Dangerous."

She let out a huff. "It's only Monday. The curse doesn't go into effect for another five days," she told him in a quiet voice so no one would overhear. If these students weren't yet aware of the curse hanging over her head, she didn't want to broadcast it. From the corner of her eye, she saw her parents alight from the coach.

"Nice helmet," someone said from behind her. "Yours?" She looked over one shoulder. It was the brown-haired boy. He held out the helmet that had rolled to his feet. Nestled on top of his wavy hair, she now noticed, was a crown. Which meant he was a prince. There were lots of those in fairy tales, of course.

"Um. Yeah. Thanks." She smiled at him as she took the helmet. "Sorry I almost trampled you a minute ago."

"S'okay. I'm fine." He stepped back a pace, looking down at the ground like he'd suddenly turned bashful. Or like he feared she might jump back on Starlight and try to run him over again!

She finger-combed her tangled hair, figuring she must look frightful after her wild ride. "You sure you're okay?"

Glancing back up at her, he nodded. Then his cheeks flushed and he rammed his hands in his pockets. "See you later, Princess Unicorn." Grinning now, he took a few more steps backward, then turned and jogged off to his friends.

"Hey —" She started to ask about the jousting team, but stopped when her mother's gloved hand took hers.

"Come along, Rose," she said, tugging her away. The footman scurried forward and took the helmet from her. After stuffing it into her trunk, he slammed the lid shut. He and the driver stacked the trunks three high, hefted them, and then started toward the school, balancing the weight between them. They would take the trunks to her room, she supposed, wherever that might be.

Still holding on to her hand as if Rose were a very small child, her mom started to lead her into the school, too. But when Rose heard a nervous whinny, she stopped and pulled away. "Starlight?"

A servant dressed in a fancy gold-and-purple suit with the GA logo on the chest had reached for her unicorn's reins to lead him off. Starlight gave another startled whinny and reared back a little.

"Wait! Where are you taking him?" Rose asked anxiously. She hitched up her blue-and-white dress a little so she wouldn't trip on its hem, and ran over to her unicorn.

"To the stables," the servant explained. Except for not being dressed in green, he looked sort of like a leprechaun, and his bushy mustache wiggled when he spoke. "Don't worry, milady. He'll be well taken care of. While you're in yon castle, he'll be brushed. And then he'll feast upon lush green grass and delicious grain, and afterward sleep in a fine stall with the Academy's ponies."

She nodded reluctantly. Although she didn't like having to part with her unicorn, she doubted very much that Starlight would be allowed to sleep in the castle with her. And she couldn't exactly sleep in the stables with him. She lay her cheek against his, wrapped both arms around his neck, and gave him a hug. "It's okay, Starlight," she reassured him. "I promised Mom and Dad I'd come here. But we won't stay long if we don't like it."

However, when Rose let him loose, he refused to go. He sidestepped the servant and thrashed his head as if to tell her, *I won't leave you!*

She stroked his muzzle. "Go make friends with the Academy ponies," she whispered to him. "I'll be fine." Finally calming, her unicorn let the servant lead him away.

Both her parents had come over when she wasn't looking. Now her mom said, "Come along, Briar Rose. Let's find the office so you can check in. Your father and I must get back to the palace soon."

They swept her away, and the three of them crossed a drawbridge over the sparkling blue river that ran beneath the school. Together, they pushed through a set of enormous wooden doors. And just like that, they were inside Grimm Academy.

2

The Danger List

*M*oments later, Rose and her parents were on the fourth floor going through a door marked OFFICE. The minute they were inside, her father's head drew back in surprise. Her mom put a perfumed handkerchief to her nose. Because it stunk like fire and brimstone in that office!

"Something's burning," Rose whispered. She peeked around her parents and spotted the office lady standing behind her desk. There was a small sign on the desk with her name on it: MS. JABBERWOCKY. The lady smiled at them, showing enormous, sharp teeth. She was green. She was scaly. She was a dragon!

Fascinating! thought Rose.

Seeing them standing there, the dragon lady held up a jar full of red and green peppers. The label on the jar said, EXTRA HOT AND SPICY.

"Callooh! Callay! Come closer, gimble family!" she called in a raspy voice. Using two clawed fingers, she pulled out three jalapeño peppers from the jar and offered them. "Snack?"

"Um, no, thanks," said Rose. Stepping between her parents, she bravely went up to the counter. "We packed finger sandwiches and berries and stuff to eat on the ride here."

"You don't know what you're missing." With that, Ms. Jabberwocky tilted her head back and opened her jaws wide. She tossed three peppers up into the air. As they dropped down again, she angled her head in quick jerks to catch each one in her open mouth. *Chomp! Chomp! Chomp!*

Rose's parents hurried forward as if to protect her from possibly being chomped by dragon teeth. She rolled her eyes. Really? It was bad enough that they'd insisted on holding her hands all the way up to the office. Oh, why did they have to treat her like such a baby?

After munching the peppers, the dragon lady washed them down with an entire bottle of hot sauce. "Ahhh!" she said, exhaling a happy, fiery breath that scorched the papers on her desktop. "Nothing like a frabjous snack. So you must be Rose? And these are your parents. We've been expecting you. Welcome! Let's get your classes set up." Whenever she pronounced the letter *P*, cinders sputtered out of her nostrils and from between her teeth. Probably the reason the office smelled like smoke.

"Yes, let's get down to business," her father, the king, insisted. "We only have a few minutes. I'm on a tight schedule."

"Rose? The list, please," her mother, the queen, reminded her.

With a sigh, Rose pulled a folded sheet of paper from her pocket. It was the Danger List. Among other dangers on it, her parents had listed all the classes that they considered too hazardous for her to take here at GA, along with the reasons why. The not-allowed list of classes began like this:

1. Siege, Catapults, and Jousts (physical education class: sharp weapons)
2. Threads (sewing class: needles)
3. Calligraphy (writing class: pointy pens)
4. Scrying (fortune-telling class: breakable crystals and mirrors, which might shatter and cause injury)

And so on, et cetera, to infinity. If this school had offered a class called Wimping Out, her parents would probably have wanted Rose to sign up for it.

She knew they only had her best interests at heart. The List was for her own good. To keep her safe from the curse written into her fairy tale in the great Books of Grimm. The one that foretold that she'd prick her finger one day and fall asleep for one hundred years. A kind fairy had told her family that this Long Nap would begin sometime after her twelfth birthday.

She brushed off that unpleasant thought. She'd packed as much adventure as she could into her life so far. As much as she could get away with, anyway. But even mild adventures would have to come to a screeching halt five days from today.

Just then a bluebird flew in through the office's high window. There was a rolled-up piece of vellum paper in its beak. Swooping low, it delivered the paper to Rose's father. Unrolling it, he quickly scanned the words written upon it. Then he looked up at Rose and her mom.

"I'm needed at the palace," he announced. Since kings were busy people, Rose wasn't really surprised that he'd been called home. He was *always* on a tight schedule. Her parents had only planned to stay until she was settled in, anyway, so she'd been expecting them to leave this evening.

After a flurry of hugs and kisses and warnings about various dangers, her parents quickly bid her farewell. And then they were gone, leaving Rose in the care of the dragon lady.

The minute the door shut behind them, a cranky new voice yelled from somewhere nearby. *"Dagnabbit!"*

Startled, Rose dropped her list of dangerous things. Her

eyes darted toward the door beyond the dragon lady's desk, from which the voice had come. The door was marked PRINCIPAL R'S OFFICE. Sounds of thumping and grumping were coming from behind it now.

"Bandersnatch! Someone's in an uffish mood," Ms. Jabberwocky commented. She shot Rose a grin. Then she became all business.

"First of all . . . classes. I've assigned them for you as I do for all new GA students, and I drew up a written sheet. Now, let's see, where is it?" She dug through the papers strewn over her desk. "Normally, I'm more organized that this, but we've been rather busy around here ever since Rapunzel found that magical straw a few weeks ago."

"Straw?" Rose bent and picked up the Danger List.

"The Straw of Gold. It's supposed to spin into unlimited amounts of gold, but so far . . ." Ms. Jabberwocky's eyes rolled toward the door marked Principal R. "Let's just say things are not going so well."

"*Stupeegrabbernatch!*" yelled the voice in the principal's office. Could that be the principal himself?

Ms. Jabberwocky made a *yikes* face, but then she said, "Never mind him." She picked up a snow globe with a tiny representation of the Academy inside it, and then set it down on a stack of ancient-looking papers like a paper-weight. Dust puffed up from the stack.

At the same time Rose handed her the Danger List. "My parents would like —" she began.

Ah-ah-a-chooo! A ball of fire shot from Ms. Jabberwocky's mouth in a humongous sneeze. When the smoke cleared, most of the Danger List was gone. No more than a scant inch of its top corner was still clasped in Ms. Jabberwocky's clawed hand. The rest of it had been burned to a crisp.

"I hope that wasn't anything tulgey important," Ms. Jabberwocky said in an apologetic tone.

"Um, no," said Rose. In fact, she felt like a huge weight had been lifted from her shoulders. The scrap of the list that was left wafted to the floor. The only word she could read on it now was, *Danger.* Rose stepped on the word, covering it with one slippered foot. Now that the list was gone, so was her need to follow it, she decided.

More banging came from the principal's office. *Thonk! Slam!* "Jabberwock*eee*!" yelled the grumpy voice.

"There in a minute, Principal R!" To Rose, Ms. Jabberwocky said, "Since I can't seem to find my assignment sheet, why don't you just choose from our list of classes? And be snicker-snack about it, please." She whipped out a large, ancient-looking book, opened it, and slid it across the desk toward Rose.

Rose stared at the list in the book for a long moment. So long, that Ms. Jabberwocky began impatiently tapping the claws of one hand on the desk. Feeling her rebellious streak suddenly kick in, she sent the dragon lady a pleasant smile. "I'll take Threads class; Calligraphy class; and Scrying class, please." Then she added firmly, "And Sieges, Catapults, and Jousts class, too."

After all, it wasn't her birthday *yet*. And although less than a week in Sieges, Catapults, and Jousts wouldn't allow her time to learn all she needed to know to become a knight, she'd still enjoy it. A lot! She'd pretend that the curse hanging over her head didn't exist. She'd forget that it meant her dream of actually becoming a knight was doomed. Till Friday, she would do whatever she wanted to. Next week, she could ask to switch to "safe" classes if she felt like the ones she'd chosen really were dangerous. No harm done.

"Got it!" The dragon lady pulled out a purple-and-gold leather-bound book and scribbled the names of Rose's chosen classes on the first blank page. "I've added a couple of additional classes to make six, but if they don't suit you, I'll bend the rules and allow you to change them later." Then, after closing the book again, she thrust it into Rose's hands. "That's your handbook."

As Rose stared down at it, an oval about two inches long suddenly appeared at the center of its cover. Right away a swirly GA logo magically drew itself inside the oval.

"Grimmawesome!" she said, watching in delight. There were so many magical things here at the Academy it seemed, far more than elsewhere in the realm.

"*Grumpsteritchysauce!* Why isn't this straw working?" yelled the voice in the other room, even louder and grumpier now. "Jabberwockeeeee!"

"Ooh, he's galumphing mad. That straw was supposed to be the answer to the Academy's financial future and . . ." Apparently deciding she'd revealed too much, Ms. Jabberwocky stopped mid-sentence.

Then she switched into super-high efficient gear. She leaned over the desk and looped a silver chain around Rose's neck. There was a long ornate key dangling from it. "Wear this from now on. It's your trunker key."

"Thank you," Rose said. She'd seen the hallway full of trunks set on their ends, and had already figured out that students must keep their belongings inside them.

Ms. Jabberwocky nodded once, and then went on. "Classes are on the first, second, and third floors. And you'll find your personal code for locking and unlocking your trunker on the first page of that handbook. Memorize the code quickly once you view it because it'll disappear forever within five minutes."

Having imparted that information, she headed for the

principal's door. "Hmm. I feel like I'm mimsy forgetting to tell you something."

"Yes, you are," said Rose. "I mean, where do I —" But her question was drowned out by the sounds of more banging and stomping from behind Principal R's door.

As the dragon lady continued walking backward toward the door, she counted on her claws: "Let's see. Trunker key, trunker code, class assignments." Behind her, the tip of her long scaly tail wrapped itself around the knob of the principal's door. The knob turned, then she slapped the door open with a *whap* of her tail.

"Oh! I know," Ms. Jabberwocky announced, snapping two clawed fingers. "Your tower task. You'll have sixth period free every Wednesday for that. Now, I must be off, *snicker-snack*! See yourself out. And have a happily-ever-after night!" She sent Rose another scary dragon-toothed grin, then stepped into the principal's office.

Rose took a quick step toward her. "Wait! Where —" she called after her, but the door to Principal R's office had already slammed shut. Quietly, she finished the question she had wanted to ask: "— do I sleep?" Her words fell into the empty room with no one to answer.

Oh well. She'd figure it out for herself. All she had to do was ask around about her trunks. Because wherever they had been taken, that's where she'd be sleeping.

A second later, Rose stepped back out into the fourth-floor hallway, holding her new handbook. She looked left and then right. Not sure where to go, she went left, back the way she and her parents had first come.

Just before she reached the stairs, she paused to admire a suit of armor standing in the hall against a wall. Its intricately carved silver lance was amazingly shiny and, well, beautiful! She reached up, wanting to test its point.

Before she could touch it, she saw something out of the corner of her eye. Three whiffs of sparkly magic had flickered in the air, back a ways toward the office. A bit of yellow, a bit of pink, a bit of purple. No! Not *them* again! She'd hoped those three wouldn't follow her here. That they'd stay behind at the palace. But no such luck. *Argh!*

The three round puffs of sparkly magic, each about the size of a melon, started to move toward her. Her eyes widened. Lickety-split, Rose took off, heading for the stairs.

Each of those magic mists contained a fairy — a chicken-yellow one, a bubble-gum pink one, and an overly curious purple one. She'd long ago realized that no one but she could see them, so she'd stopped mentioning them for fear people would think she'd gone bonkers.

After making it to the grand staircase, she wrapped both arms around her handbook, hopped on the banister, and slid all the way down, down, down to the first floor.

Her parents didn't allow her to do such things back at the palace, but she'd sneaked enough times that she'd become a pretty expert banister-slider. She was grinning when reached the bottom to land right in front of a girl standing there. A girl with long green hair that grew like curly leafy vines from her head.

"Hi!" they said at the same time, which made the girl giggle. "You're Princess Briar Rose, right?" the girl asked.

"Just Rose," said Rose.

The girl nodded. "I'm Princess Pea. But everyone just calls me Pea. Like the vegetable. C'mon. Dorms are on six. We'll be sharing." She looped an arm through Rose's and they set off back up the staircase together.

Rose couldn't believe she'd run into her assigned roommate first thing. Now *that* was a stroke of luck! Plus, she seemed friendly.

When they reached the twisty stairs again on the fourth floor, Rose paused to peek down the hall. No sign of the fairies or their sparkly mists. Breathing a sigh of relief, she jogged upward after Pea, heading for the dorms. The stairs dead-ended at two doors on the sixth-floor landing. One was emerald green and one was pearly white. Pea pulled the emerald one open. It took them to an outdoor stone walkway that ran between the towers. Outside, the night was cool and the sky was a dark, velvety blue.

When they heard splashing somewhere below, Pea stopped to lean over the wall and wave down at someone. "Night, Mermily!"

Rose looked over, too. One floor below them in a court-yard between the fifth-floor dorm towers stood a tall, three-tiered fountain. There was a mermaid about their age swimming in its waters!

Far, far below the fountain courtyard, the waters of the Once Upon River lapped against the bottom of the castle's stone dungeon. And above their heads the pointy tops of the three towers seemed to rise high enough to poke the puffy night clouds.

"Does that mermaid girl sleep in the fountain?" asked Rose as she and Pea continued along the walkway.

Pea nodded. "Usually. She's Cinda's roomie over in Pearl dorm. Cinda, as in Cinderella, that is. I used to live in Pearl, too, but then I got switched to Emerald. All the tow-ers have jewel nicknames," she went on, pointing. "The ones on our side of the Academy are Pearl, Ruby, and Emerald."

Rose looked at the pearly white, dazzling red, and green towers, the last one gleaming in the darkness like spar-kling, lush green grass.

"The boys' towers are Onyx, Topaz, and Zircon," Pea added, waving a hand toward Gray Castle on the opposite end of the school.

It turned out that Emerald Tower was circular and was ringed with little bedrooms, all set along the outer stone wall, each with a decorative curtain as an entrance. In the center of the tower there was a gathering space with a fireplace hearth that appeared to be made of real emerald jewels! Surrounding it were a half-dozen comfy chairs and a few tables. One of them was long and rectangular with green felt on top — it was a pool table. And scattered around the floor were a bunch of throw cushions in various shades of green, turquoise, and blue.

"In here," said Pea, pulling aside the curtain-door to their alcove. Inside, a cute green-striped oval rug lay in the center of the floor. On the far wall beyond the rug was a big, single window with round glass panes. Canopy beds with swooping swags of wispy see-through fabric draped across the top stood on either side of the room. To see the canopies well, Rose had to stand on tiptoe since both beds were raised about six feet off the floor on tall bedposts. *Uh oh,* she thought in dismay. This could be a problem. A problem that had nothing to do with the dangers of sharp objects, however.

"That's your side," Pea informed her, following her gaze.

"Thanks," said Rose, smiling at her. At the end of each bed stood an armoire with mirrored doors and a ladder.

She climbed halfway up hers to look at her bed. She smoothed a hand over the coverlet. It was her favorite color, lavender.

She glanced over at the comforter on Pea's bed. It had green dots. She wondered if the dots were supposed to be peas. It would make sense in a weird sort of way!

Seeing Rose's expression, Pea told her, "I know what you must be thinking. The Academy is grimmazing. But the beds are terrible. So *not* comfy. I don't sleep a wink."

Rose nodded, though she hadn't been thinking any such thing. Besides, no matter how uncomfy the mattress, if the curse in her tale ever came true she'd sleep for a hundred years, which was *far* longer than a wink. However, she'd worry about all that five days from now. In the meantime, she had big plans for her final days of pre-birthday freedom. And they didn't include trying to play things safe.

However, this bed was kind of dangerous if you were the kind of princess who sometimes went sleepwalking. Which she was. She hadn't done that in a long time, though. So maybe it wouldn't be a problem here.

Just then, Pea gave a huge yawn. "I'm pooped," she said. "Mind if I hit the sack?"

"No, I mean, that's fine with me." After Pea gave her some directions, Rose slipped out of their room and found the alcove marked WASHING UP. There, she bathed and put on pj's. By the time she got back, Pea was asleep.

Rose found her three trunks, which had been stashed beside her under-the-bed desk. Not wanting to wake Pea, she tiptoed around as she put things away. Back home in the palace, she had a huge room all to herself, so sharing this small room was going to take some getting used to.

As she unpacked, she heard faint laughter and clanking sounds coming from somewhere outside. Glancing out the window between her and Pea's beds she saw those four girls again. Cinda and her friends. They were laughing and playing putt-putt golf on the "green" atop the long hall that connected the Pink and Gray castles.

But what really caught her eye was the group of boys at the far end of the green, closer to Gray Castle. The ones from the jousting team. They were sword fighting!

Just as she decided to go down and ask to join them, however, all the students on the green ended their games. Then they went inside, boys into Gray Castle and girls into Pink Castle.

Oh, grumblemonkeys, thought Rose. However, maybe it was best that she not rush to make friends around here. She didn't want to get a reputation as pushy. And if she somehow managed to outwit the curse, her parents might summon her home, anyway.

After a while, she began to yawn, so she, too, climbed into bed. She quickly fell asleep . . . and was soon dreaming a sort of dream she'd never had before. A dream that almost felt *real*, though she knew it couldn't be.

In her dream she was a knight! With a sword. She was using it to fight someone. Someone evil. *Clank! Clank!*

"Attention, students of Grimm Academy! Breakfast begins in one hour."

Wrenched from sleep, Rose sat straight up. Her heart was racing, her breath coming in gasps. She'd never even held a sword before. Weapons were pretty much number one no-nos on her parents' Danger List. But her dream had seemed so real.

She looked around woozily. *Wait!* Where was she? Not in bed, that was for sure. This room wasn't familiar in the least.

She was sitting in a big, tufted leather chair before a large antique desk. High along the wall above it was a speaker through which the voices had blared the break-fast announcement. The rest of the walls around her were lined with bookshelves and stuffed with oddball things.

Dozens of portraits, including seven in carved golden frames hung on the wall directly behind her.

And — *Oh no!* — she was still wearing her pj's. So that's how she'd gotten here. She'd been sleepwalking. Again. *Argh!*

3

Taking a Leap

At least there were no sparkly pink, yellow, and purple mist puff fairies floating anywhere in the room to annoy her, thought Rose. There were, however, some beautiful quill feather pens lying in a wooden box on top of the desk. A stack of vellum paper lay beside the box. To her surprise, the stack suddenly magically lifted itself to hover about four feet above the desk.

Swish! Rose gasped as it began scattering itself. Soon, sheets of paper were flying around the room like a deck of cards being dealt wildly into the air by unseen hands.

After several sheets drifted to settle on the desktop, one of the pens hopped out of the wooden box and flew across them to land in her hand. Startled, she dropped it and leaped from her chair, then stared as the pen skated around the desk, scribbling aimlessly on the sheets of paper.

"Hello? Are you a magic pen?" she asked it after a moment. The quill pen stopped scribbling and the tip of its feathers bobbed up and down at her, as if nodding yes.

"Besides scribbling on your own, can you do other kinds of magic?" she asked it.

Instantly, the pen was off again. But now it wrote words: *That's for me to know and you to find out.*

What a cheeky little pen! she thought. Fascinated, she picked it up and drew a few lines with it on the sheet of paper. "Sorry, I can't really draw. That's supposed to be a flower." Quick as a wink, her drawing rearranged itself into a beautiful rose, complete with thorny stem.

"Why, that's exactly the flower I meant to draw. How did you know?" Before it could write a reply, Rose was startled by a sound.

Whoosh! She turned in time to see a large book fly from a shelf and land in the middle of the stone floor. *Whap!* Its pages fell open to a fairy tale. She set the pen down and went to stare at it, reading the title aloud, *"Rumpelstiltskin."*

As the word rolled off her tongue every object in the room seemed to rustle, moving around a little nervously. *Weird!*

Rose rubbed her eyes. And when she looked again, nothing was moving. "Maybe it was just my imagination," she murmured. Except the pen was definitely moving again on its own. She went over to the desk to see what it had written: *Never speak the principal's name.*

"You mean, 'Rumpelstiltskin'?" she asked it. In response, the rustling in the room happened again, even more nervous-sounding this time. So it hadn't been her imagination after all!

"Sorry, but why not?" she asked the pen. But it had gone still now and lay on the desk unmoving, just like any normal pen.

She let out a perplexed huff. "Okay, be that way, you silly pen," she told it.

With that, she left the desk and went over to look out the room's only door. She appeared to be in some kind of warehouse with shelves and shelves of storage. She looked down at her slipperless feet, then over at the pen.

"Where am I, anyway?" she asked it. Nothing. She'd been hoping it might write the answer to her question.

Hearing a boinging noise, she swung around to see that a half-dozen balls the size of oranges had leaped from a box on a shelf. After hitting the floor and bouncing upward, they began juggling themselves in midair! Not only that, now some school supplies — an eraser, a pair of scissors, a bottle of glue, and about a dozen paperclips — hopped from another box to begin fighting a comical battle on the floor. She watched the scissors warily as they occasionally sprang into the air, but they didn't seem to mean her any harm, despite their sharpness.

Just then, something drifted down from the room's ceiling to land butterfly-soft on her nose. Startled, Rose slapped it away, then saw that it was only a slip of paper. Before she could bend down to read the words on it, the scissors zipped over and snipped it into a dozen pieces.

"Thanks a lot!" she scolded. She kneeled to rearrange the pieces, but all she could read were three words: *Tower Task: Candles*. She remembered Ms. Jabberwocky saying something about a task she'd have to do on Wednesdays, sixth period.

"Candles. What kind of task is that?" she asked aloud. But no one answered, and the pen remained still. She reached for the rest of the tiny pieces of paper nearby, when suddenly, the glue decided to squirt itself at the paperclips. *Blurp!* A big glob of glue sprayed out and the rest of the paper pieces got sloppy wet. Standing, she crammed the three dry pieces of paper with the words she'd read into the pocket of her pj's.

Choo! Choo! In a corner of the room a toy train started chugging along a track. In fact, all around her, more objects had begun to move under their own power. When a snow globe lifted from a shelf and headed her way, she quickly backed against a wall to avoid getting bonked. However it seemed to somehow know she was there. It circled carefully around her and gradually came to rest in the outstretched hand of a stone statue standing across the room.

Rose gaped in astonishment. "This is one bizarro room!" she blurted. She decided to leave. But in the doorway, she paused, glancing down at the pj's she wore.

"Hope I don't run into anyone," she murmured to herself. Then she stepped out the door. Determined to figure out where she was exactly, she wandered up and down the aisles she'd glimpsed earlier. This place reminded her of the maze in the grand garden back home. Only instead of high green hedges, this maze was made of shelves. Shelves that stretched so far into the distance she could see no end to them. There were rows upon rows of them and little rooms filled with who knew what. Tons of books, for one thing, but other stuff, too. Then it flashed on her. This must be the Grimmstone Library!

Everyone in Grimmlandia had heard of it. For it held the legendary Books of Grimm, written by the two Grimm brothers, Jacob and Wilhelm. They'd built this Academy not just for all the students who attended GA, but also to protect their amazing collection of books, as well as enchanted artifacts from various tales and nursery rhymes.

Flap! Flap! Looking up, Rose saw snow-white geese. They were flapping their wings and zooming back and forth high overhead, expertly navigating among chandeliers lit with dozens of candles that hung from the ceiling. A net bag dangled from each goose's bright orange beak. Some of the bags held books. Others held objects, such as harmonicas, jars of buttons, balls of yarn, and fashionable hats.

None of the geese paid any attention to her as she walked the aisles between the shelves, gazing around in wonder. The library's wares appeared to be arranged in alphabetical order. She passed jars of mustard and stacks of mud pies sitting alongside books by *M* authors in Section *M*. In Section *L*, she passed bags of lollipops, boxes of lost things, and stacks of love letters tied together with ribbons of long lace.

From the corner of one eye, she spied a ladder leaning against the shelf of letters. She scrambled up it to stand atop the eight-foot-tall shelves. As usual, she didn't consider the danger of doing such a thing until after she'd done it. *Oops.* Good thing her parents weren't here to see her now.

The top of the shelving unit turned out to be a great vantage point for gazing across the sea of other shelves that made up this enormous library. She walked along the top of the shelf she'd climbed, hoping she was going in the right direction to eventually reach the library's entrance. She needed to get back to the dorm and get ready for classes!

Swoosh! A dark shadow fell over her. She looked up to see something huge flying overhead.

Flap! Flap! It was another goose. Only this one was as big as a horse. A woman wearing a frilly white cap, a crisp white apron, and spectacles was riding on its back.

After nearly toppling off the shelf in surprise, Rose quickly dropped to a crouch to regain her balance. "Hello? Which way is the exit?" she called up to the woman. But she didn't hear, and the goose flapped on past.

"*Oh, dust bunnies*," Rose grumped under her breath.

"What are you doing up there?" asked a voice from below.

Whirling around, she looked down to see two boys standing below in the aisle. The three of them all gaped at one another for a few seconds without speaking. She wasn't sure who looked more surprised. Them or her.

One was the same brown-haired jousting boy she'd nearly knocked down yesterday, she realized. The one who'd returned her helmet. Running into him again seemed a coincidence, to be sure.

Suddenly remembering she was in her pj's, Rose felt her cheeks redden. Horribly embarrassed, she blurted out the first random thing that popped into her mind. "Are girls allowed on the jousting team?"

"Huh?" Both boys gave her confused looks.

"Because I want to try out. Think about it. Talk later!" They probably thought she was completely loopy, she decided as she leaped across a three-foot gap onto the top of the next shelf over. And maybe they were right!

She leaped across the next gap and onto another shelf top, and onto the next, and the next. She knew she was taking chances since she could fall to the floor and break a leg (or worse) if one of her leaps missed. But she couldn't seem to stop with the daredevil act.

Her fairytale curse was always in the back of her mind, spurring her on to take chances like this before she turned twelve and had to behave. Despite the sheltered life she'd lived at the family palace, her overprotective parents hadn't been able to keep an eye on her every minute of every day. So whenever she'd been out from under their watchful eyes she'd gone wild, doing crazy things that made her heart pound with excitement.

Once, she'd jumped from the top of a crenellated wall into the moat down below. She'd jumped fences with Starlight. And she'd climbed the tallest trees in the forest behind the palace to swing from vine to vine.

Just then, she came to a break in the shelves that was far too wide to leap, and she skidded to a halt. Her arms windmilled as she teetered forward at the edge of the shelftop on which she still stood. Luckily, she found her balance again and didn't go crashing down to her doom. Farther ahead, she saw what could be the exit.

As she was contemplating how to get there, two girls appeared in the aisle below her. One was wearing a tiara with blue-green stones and the other a red cape. They were friends of that girl she'd nearly trampled, Cinda.

"Hey! Up here!" she called softly down to them.

The two girls looked up, and Red Cape immediately asked the same question the boys had. "What are you doing up there?"

"Shh! Long story," Rose said quietly. She looked around, but didn't see anyone else besides the two girls. By now, she'd left those boys far behind.

Dropping to her hands and knees atop the shelf, she asked, "Which way is out?"

Both girls pointed in a direction diagonally across the huge room. Her heart sank. She wasn't near the exit after all. It would take way too much shelf-hopping to make it to where they pointed. She eyed the girls again. "Any ideas on how I can get down?"

"Too bad Rapunzel isn't here. She could probably stretch her magic comb charm into a ladder," said Red Cape. "There are real ladders in the *L* section, though."

Tiara girl glanced up at her. "I'm Snow," she said.

"Red," added the other girl.

When Rose looked confused, Red-Cape girl grinned, adding, "Those are our names."

"Oh." Rose grinned back. "Sorry, I was thinking of the kind of snow that falls and the color red, so I didn't — . Anyway, I'm Rose, like the flower. So can you help me?"

"We're closer to Section *S* for stairs than to *L* for ladders," Snow told her. Pointing, she added, "*S* is that way. Only you'd have to jump three aisles to get there, and that'd be pretty dangerous. So maybe —"

Before Snow could finish, Rose started leaping. The two Grimm girls dashed to follow, anxiously staring up at her antics the whole time.

"This is crazy!" fretted Snow.

"You could fall!" exclaimed Red, stating the obvious.

Fortunately, Rose reached the *S* section safely. "Aha! Stairs." Sure enough, a set of steps led from a shelf to the floor. She started to take them down. But then she spotted an enormous shoe farther down the shelf she was standing on. It was as tall as the shelf, and so long that several shelves across from it had been removed to make room for its toe. And it had little windows and a door!

"What's that?" she asked the two Grimm girls, who'd caught up and now stood below.

"It belongs to the Old Woman Who Lived in a Shoe," replied Snow. "She had so many children she didn't know what to do."

"So she moved from this too-small shoe house, which she stowed here in the library, into an even bigger shoe house instead," said Red. "At least, that's what I heard."

While they talked, Rose sat on the edge of the shelf, poised at the top of the shoe, which was tall and really more like a boot. Pushing off, she slid down its sloping top all the way to its toe. When she landed on the floor, she laughed. "Wow! It might not have been that great of a house, but it makes a cool slide!"

Snow and Red stared at her, stunned looks on their faces. Rose grinned at them and wiggled her eyebrows. "Sorry. I know that was kind of risky. Couldn't resist, though. It was fun!"

"Yeah, well, I'm glad you're okay," said Snow.

Red nodded. "What were you doing up on those shelves, anyway? And, um, why are you in pj's?"

Rose sighed, shifting from one bare foot to the other. "I sleepwalk sometimes," she finally admitted, shrugging. "It happened last night and I woke up here in the library. I didn't know where I was, so I climbed the shelves to look for the exit."

"How awful!" Snow sympathized. "About the sleep-walking, I mean."

"Worst thing is that now I'll have to walk through the halls in my pj's," said Rose. "Which will be majorly grimmbarrassing. How far is it from here to the dorms?"

"Library's on the first floor today," Red told her.

"So that'll mean five sets of stairs up to get to the dorms," added Snow. The two girls went on to explain how the library magically moved around the various floors of the Academy each day. And how sometimes it shrank itself as small as a closet, while at other times it made itself even bigger than it was now — bigger than the Academy itself! Yet it always managed to fit wherever it put itself.

Cool! thought Rose.

"I'd fetch you a gown, but I don't think it would fit in my basket," said Red. Rose had no idea what she meant by that. Was her basket magic or something? Before she could ask, Red snapped her fingers and looked over at Snow. "I know! We can get her a gown to wear from Section *G*."

"Perfect!" Snow told Rose, bouncing on her toes. "Then you won't have to wander around in your pj's! We'll have to hurry up about it if we want to get to breakfast on time, though. Let's go!"

As the three girls headed off together, Red looked over her shoulder at Rose. "Hey, I just remembered something.

The library doorknob always asks a riddle before it'll let you in. So if you were asleep, how did you get in?"

Rose shrugged. "No idea." But then she vaguely recalled sleepily talking to a beaked doorknob. One without the customary GA logo on it. "Oh, wait. Um, I think I *was* asked a riddle. By some kind of chicken-headed knob."

"Gooseknob," both Grimm girls corrected.

Rose nodded, her forehead wrinkling as she searched her memory for that fragment of her dream. At last she said, "Got it! The riddle went like this: 'I am at the beginning of every end, at the end of every middle, and in the middle of every dream. What am I?'"

"Hmm. That's a tough one," said Red, wrinkling her nose.

Snow nodded. "So what was the answer?"

Rose grinned and pointed to a sign in the section they were passing through. It read: Section *E*.

"Oh, I get it," said Snow. "The answer to the riddle is the letter *e*."

"Pr*EEE*cisely," said Rose. Which made them all giggle.

When they reached the *G* section they came upon a tiny mirror, which was no bigger than a three-inch square. It hung in the middle of a large otherwise empty wall. As Rose watched, Red and Snow both gently tugged outward on the four corners of the mirror's silver frame.

The mirror began to stretch larger, until it was taller and wider than they were! And then it spoke to them:

"What do you wish?
You need only to ask,
And I will complete for you
Any fair task."

Red replied:

"Mirror, Mirror, at aisle's end,
Please make a gown for our new friend."

Snow nudged Rose with an elbow. "Tell the mirror what you want it to look like," she prompted.

"Um, an everyday gown for class?" Rose requested vaguely.

"What's your favorite color?" Red asked.

"Lavender," said Rose.

Flip-flap! As her words died away, a dozen bluebirds came flying toward the girls from across the library. Their beaks held bedsheet-size pieces of a beautiful lavender fabric that billowed out behind them like colorful sails. They carried scissors, pins, and thread as well. The birds swooped down beside Rose, wrapped the fabric around her, and got to work.

In no time at all, she stood before the mirror clad in a finished gown. Ribbons were tied just so and tiny sparkly gems along her calf-length hem winked in the chandeliers' light from overhead.

"Wow!" Rose said softly. She'd had pretty dresses before, but never one whipped up in mere minutes by blue-birds. Snow had even gotten slippers for her from another aisle to match! She swayed from side to side, studying herself in the glass and enjoying how the skirt of her gown swished. "It's beautiful."

At her words, the mirror must've decided its job was complete. It began to slowly shrink, then snapped back to its original small size.

Red nodded toward Rose's pj's, where they lay on the floor. "Want me to send those to your dorm room for you? Just put them in here." She patted her cute wicker basket.

As the birds had begun to work, Rose had barely noticed when her pj's had disappeared from under the gown. Somehow, they'd wound up on the floor. When she plucked them up now, three tiny pieces of paper fell out of their pocket.

"What's that?" asked Snow, pointing to them.

Rose kneeled and gathered up the pieces along with her pj's, then stood again. "It's my tower task assignment, I think. Long story, but the paper it was written on got cut up by some crazy scissors in the room where I woke up."

"You got a tower task already? What is it?" asked Snow, seeming unsurprised about the crazy scissors part. Magic like that must be far more commonplace in GA than in the rest of Grimmlandia, Rose figured.

"Making candles? At least I think so," said Rose.

Red lifted her basket's lid. After Rose set her pj's inside it, the lid dropped shut. Then Red commanded, "A tisket a tasket, *send these pj's to Rose's room*, basket."

When Red opened the basket afterward it was empty. "Those pj's should be in your alcove when you get back tonight."

"Thanks! I wondered if your basket might be magic," Rose said, impressed. "Very cool."

Red just smiled, and nodded. "It followed me from Drama class one day, wanting to be mine. C'mon. We'd better get going."

As they headed off again, Snow asked Red, "Do you think Rose's tower task might have something to do with the candlestick-maker in the 'Rub-A-Dub-Dub' nursery rhyme?"

"Huh?" said Rose. *What is she talking about?* "I'm not really into making candles," she protested. "Do you think maybe I could trade for a different task?"

Snow looked doubtful.

"We're each given a specific task for a reason," Red said encouragingly. "Somehow, candles will turn out right for you. You'll see. Over in Pearl Tower, Cinda's the Hearthkeeper, I'm the Snackmaker, and Snow is Tidy-upper."

"And, *mmm*," said Snow, rubbing her stomach. "I can tell you that Red makes the best cookies in Grimmlandia!"

"Well, I just hope Ms. Jabberwocky and her tower-task givers know what they're *frabjous snicker-snack* doing, giving me this particular task." The other two girls laughed at her creative use of some of Ms. Jabberwocky's favorite words.

Before they left the *G* section completely, Red and Snow stopped off at a bookshelf filled with Grimm fairy-tale books.

"Just a sec. Snow and I need to check on something," Red explained. Then the two girls each pulled a different book from the shelf and opened them to begin skimming a few pages. The books they held looked very old, and were bound with fine leather covers stamped with fancy gold lettering and old-fashioned swirly gold decorations.

"Mine's okay," said Snow after a couple of minutes.

"Mine, too," said Red with obvious relief. "But we should ask Cinda and Rapunzel, too. They were going to check their fairy tales earlier this morning."

Rose tilted her head. "I don't get it. What were you looking for?"

The other two Grimm girls shot each other looks as they replaced their books. Then, as if deciding they could trust her, Snow said, "There's been trouble here at GA. A certain evil society —"

"One that calls itself Exceptional Villains In Literature — E.V.I.L., for short — has hinted that they hope to change the fairy tales around," Red continued. "You know, make the evil characters more important. Stuff like that. So we were checking our tales to make sure there'd been no changes to them."

Rose gasped. "Wow! Who has that kind of magical power?" Her mind boggled. Then, before the girls could reply, she thought of something. "Hey, you know that room I woke up in this morning? It was weirdly magical, with all kinds of stuff that sailed through the air. Including a book of Grimm fairy tales that flew off the shelf, and opened itself to the *Rumpelstiltskin* tale."

Both girls' eyes went wide, and Snow put a finger to her lips. "Shh! Never say his name!" she whispered.

"Oops, sorry," Rose replied, whispering as well. "That's what the pen said, er, *wrote*, too."

"What pen?" asked Red.

Before Rose could reply, Snow said, "That room you were in. Did it have a big desk and lots of portraits hanging on the wall?"

Rose nodded.

Looking somewhat alarmed, Red said to Snow, "That sounds like the Grimm brothers' room. Maybe we'd better go over there and see what's up."

"Yeah! Quick, though," said Snow. "Or else we'll miss breakfast." With that, all three girls headed back to where Rose had awakened that morning.

4

Evil Editing

Once back inside the magical room, Rose saw that the Grimm brothers' book that had flown off the shelf earlier was now in place again, instead of lying on the floor where she'd last seen it. And the magic pen now lay unmoving in its box. All was calm.

"That book was on the floor, I promise!" said Rose. "And all sorts of stuff in here was acting up."

"We believe you," said Red. "Things move around in here. Happens all the time."

Snow pulled out the book containing the principal's fairy tale and set it on the desk. "Yeah. This room is the most magical place in the whole Academy," she told Rose. "Lots of strange things happen here. In fact, Cinda once saw a nose and eyeball poke, er, *peek* out of that heraldry shield above the desk. And another time, she and Rapunzel saw an arm reach out!" She shivered and pointed to the spot.

Red had been leafing through the book Snow had set on the desk. Now she began to read the *Rumpelstiltskin* tale aloud. Even though she added an impressive amount of extra drama to her voice, the tale sounded somehow boring and . . . *wrong.* Not at all how Rose remembered it.

"So Principal R tried and tried to spin the straw into gold, but the foolish little man failed because he was no good at it" — Red read with a frown — *"and then many others tried to spin the straw into gold. Including the illustrious and beautiful-beyond-compare Ms. Wicked."* The next couple of pages were blank, so she skipped over them to read the three words on the tale's final page, *"To be continued."*

"Oh, no!" Snow breathed, as she and Rose stepped closer to gaze at the open book. "That's not how the story goes."

"Yeah, it's all different, and what's up with these blank pages?" Rose wondered.

"E.V.I.L." Red and Snow said at the same time, sounding horrified and maybe also a little scared.

"Somehow, they've done this," said Red. She looked at Snow. "I have a feeling that whether or not your stepmom succeeds at spinning the straw, the E.V.I.L. Society will write that she did. They seem to want her to star in this fairy tale, not Principal R."

Snow's eyes widened in horror. "If this new, wrong version of the tale somehow gets into all the fairy-tale books, over time everyone might forget that it's totally wrong!"

"Your stepmom's named Ms. Wicked?" asked Rose. She had a bunch of questions swirling in her head about what these girls had said, but that was the first one that popped out.

Snow nodded. "She teaches Scrying here at the Academy."

"But I don't get it. The straw in the fairy tale is supposed to get spun into gold by Rumpelstiltskin, right?" said Rose.

All the objects in the room grew restless at the mention of his name. The toy train began chugging around the room again, a ball and some jacks began playing a game together, and a tiny ballerina began to dance to the tinkling music inside its open jewelry box.

"Shh! You really have to stop saying the principal's name," cautioned Red. "Rule 37 in the handbook. Just use a nickname instead."

"That's what we do," said Snow. "Like Stiltsky or His Principalship. Cinda calls him Grumpystiltskin."

"And Wolfgang calls him the Rumpster," added Red.

In spite of their troubles, Rose couldn't help giggling. "Okay, okay. Guess I better read up on the Academy rules."

She hoped there wasn't one about not walking and leaping across library shelves. Or one that forbade sleepwalking.

Scrunching her nose in puzzlement, she gazed over Red's shoulder again at the *Rumpelstiltskin* story, which was now a mere page long. "Here's something I don't get. Whoever rewrote this tale stuck Snow's stepmom into the story with no explanation at all for how she got there. And the plot — what little there is of it — jumps all around. Also, the end doesn't explain anything. It just drifts off. Why is it so badly written?"

Red and Snow exchanged glances and Rose had a feeling they were holding something back from her.

Choo! Choo! She did a little hop up over the train that was still whizzing around as it came toward her. "C'mon. What do you know that I don't?" she asked the other two girls.

Red hesitated slightly before pointing to one of the portraits on the wall. "See that guy? He's a Grimm brother, too. Jacob and Wilhelm banished him from Grimmlandia long ago, and now he's pretty much the head of E.V.I.L. His name is Ludwig."

She paused as the objects in the room began rustling again. Apparently they didn't like anyone saying his name *or* Rumpelstiltskin's name aloud. This time, however, their movements sounded different, more *scared* than upset. A jack-in-the-box began popping in and out of its box, a glass fell over and shattered, a toy turtle pulled its head and feet into its shell, and a plant suddenly withered. Then the whole room went wild, with things flying and bouncing around.

"Let's get out of here!" yelled Snow, dodging several books that had flown off a shelf while also trying to be heard over the din. She didn't have to suggest it twice. The girls raced from the room, out of the library, and down the school stairs.

As they ran, Snow and Red explained to Rose how artifacts had been stolen from the library a short time ago. And that they'd somehow been used to make loopholes in the tales, which now allowed stories to be rewritten.

"We only got the artifacts back a few weeks ago after foiling the witch from Rapunzel's tale," said Snow.

"Just in the nick of time, too," added Red. "Getting them back stopped Ludwig from worming his way into Grimmlandia . . . for now."

When they finally reached the first-floor hallway, they heard a clock bonging the half hour.

"Oh, good. At least something's going right this morning," said Snow, sounding breathless from their rushed escape. "It's only seven-thirty. Which means we were only in the library for five minutes, library time. It's still breakfast."

"*Five minutes?* But how can that be? Surely we were in there way longer than that," said Rose.

"Time can go faster or slower inside the library than time outside it," Red explained. "C'mon. Let's get over to the Great Hall and eat."

Minutes later, Rose was gazing around in awe at the long, long room they'd just entered. The Great Hall was magnificent! Easily ten times the size of the dining hall back home. There was a balcony at each end, rows of windows with beautiful diamond-shaped glass panes, and colorful banners draped on the walls. Some of the windows were propped open, and birds flew in and out, crossing in from one side and zooming back out the other. Running the length of the Hall on either side were long linen-draped tables with benches. Students eating breakfast filled most of the spaces along them but there were a few empty spots left.

Red and Snow's two friends from yesterday morning waved them over. They had saved seats for Red and Snow, and now also made room for Rose next to Cinda, the candle-flame-yellow-haired girl.

"Hi, I'm Cinda," Cinda told Rose.

"And I'm Rapunzel," said the goth girl Rose had seen out on the lawn with the other three girls.

Rose nodded, having already figured that out. "Nice to meet you."

"But everyone's been wondering who you are," Cinda went on. "I mean, we know your name is Briar Rose, since it was announced yesterday that you'd be coming. But we don't know your fairy tale."

"Please. Call me Rose." It surprised her that none of them seemed to have made the connection that Briar Rose was the same person as Sleeping Beauty. Did that mean *no one* here at the school knew that she was Sleeping Beauty yet? Perhaps not even the principal? Well, if that was the case, she wasn't about to spread the news. Because if she did, everyone might start worrying about her overly much, like people back home at the palace did. And she could live without that!

So she simply fluttered her hand in a casual gesture. "Oh, my tale's a minor one and not very well known," she fibbed. "Hardly worth the telling, really."

"I'm starving," Red announced right then, thankfully changing the subject. She reached toward one of the many identical platters placed at intervals along the center of their long table. Each platter was piled with tiny, one-inch square waffles. Small, clean silver plates were stacked beside the platters. A sign on the waffle platter nearest them said TAKE ONE.

One teeny waffle? That's all we get for breakfast? wondered Rose. Like Red, she was starving!

"Ooh! Never-ending waffles. *Grimmyummy!*" exclaimed Snow from across the table. She and Red each took a small plate, forked up one tiny waffle apiece, and dropped the waffles onto their plates.

Copying them, Rose did the same. After setting her plate before her, she poured syrup over her miniature waffle and ate it in one bite. *Well, that was a nice snack,* she thought. But she was still hungry. Luckily, when she looked back down at her plate, there was another tiny waffle sitting there. So she ate that one, too. Then yet another one appeared on her silver plate. No matter how many of the tasty, little squares she ate, more appeared.

She grinned to herself. *Duh.* Now she got it. That's why these waffles were called "never-ending."

After she'd eaten a few of the waffle squares, too, Red flourished her cape dramatically and looked around, as if to make sure no enemy was watching. "There's trouble in the library. In the Grimm brothers' room," she announced to Cinda and Rapunzel.

Snow leaned over and whispered in Rose's ear. "Red's in drama class. She was the lead in the last school play."

Rose whispered back, "Why am I not surprised?" She and Snow shared a grin.

Then the girls all leaned their heads close together over

the table so that Red and Snow could explain how the *Rumpelstiltskin* tale had been changed.

"You say the book with his altered tale was in the Grimm brothers' room?" Cinda asked when they finished the telling. Red, Snow, and Rose all nodded.

"But not even Ludwig himself has been able to get into that room!" Rapunzel exclaimed.

"Yes, but I saw him *trying* to on my first day at the Academy, remember?" said Cinda. "Even though that room repels evil, he managed to poke his nose in through the shield over the desk."

"But that was as far as he got," said Rapunzel. "So if he can't get in, how did a tale *inside* the room get changed? Unless maybe it got changed while it was out in the main part of the library, and the book was put in the room later?"

"All I know is, if changes can happen there, they can happen *anywhere*," said Snow.

Just then Pea came up to the table and sat down in the empty space on Rose's other side. "Hey, you left your handbook in our room," she said, passing Rose the book Ms. Jabberwocky had given her the day before.

"Oh, thanks. I forgot all about it," said Rose.

"Where'd you go so early this morning, anyway?" Pea went on. She took a silver plate and a tiny waffle for herself, and began eating.

"The library," Rose replied truthfully. She was saved from having to explain further when trumpets suddenly blared. *Ta-ta-ta-ta-ta-ta-tum!*

She jumped at the sound. Along with everyone else, she glanced up to see that two musicians had appeared on the second-floor balcony at the far west end of the two-story Great Hall. Having gotten everyone's attention, the musicians lowered their long, thin, golden trumpets.

A wide wooden shelf hung high on the stone wall behind them, she noticed. And a row of five knights' helmets forged of shiny iron sat upon it. Each had a different-colored decorative feather sticking up from its top. As she watched, their visors suddenly began moving, making faint creaking and clanking sounds.

"Attention, scholars!" they chorused in formal-sounding voices. "All rise for today's announcements from the great and goodly principal of Grimm Academy!"

Rose's jaw dropped. *Those helmet-heads were speaking!* The students all rose dutifully and turned toward the balcony. So she did likewise.

Stomp! Stomp! First the top of the principal's tall hat appeared above the balcony railing. Then more hat. Then a face with a long nose and a long chin below it. Finally, his head and shoulders appeared. He was a gnome! Three feet tall at most.

The principal began announcements. She recognized his voice from her visit to the office this morning. Though he was small, his voice wasn't. It carried the full length of the Hall. "We have three orders of business this morning," he began. "Firstly, a reminder that the Grimmstone Library Games are this Saturday."

Pea leaned over and whispered to Rose, "Happens every year in the library. There'll be strength contests like hefting stacks of books. And dust-the-shelf relay races. Jousting in Section *J*. That kind of stuff. It's basically a way to get the library cleaned up once a year. But it's pretty fun."

Rose's ears had perked up at the jousting part. "Cool, thanks," she whispered back.

Because she'd been talking with Pea, she missed some of what the principal had said. But she caught the last part.

". . . Briar Rose, please move to the center of the Hall and introduce yourself!"

Setting her handbook on the floor by her chair, Rose stood and confidently marched to the center of the Hall. There, she smiled at everyone, and told them her name in a clear, calm voice, just as her elocution tutor had taught her to do back home. "How do you do. I'm Briar Rose of Thorn Palace in the southeastern part of the realm of Grimmlandia. Please, do call me Rose."

Ping! Ping! Ping! Suddenly, those three puffs of magical mist appeared, one on either side of her head and one in front of her face. *Oh no! Not now!*

From within the puffs, three small fairy voices began making suggestions that only she could hear. Unwanted suggestions, as usual.

"Curtsey again to show off your adorable gown," advised the fairy from the pink mist on her left side.

"No! She might trip. And hit her head on one of these sharp stone-floor tiles," the fairy in the chicken-yellow mist cautioned. It was on her right side.

"Hey, who's that cute boy over there?" asked the purple one. Rose glanced over to see the brown-haired boy from the library. Jousting Boy is what she'd named him in her head. And now she murmured the nickname.

"Huh? What kind of name is that?" the purple-mist fairy asked.

"Just go back to your seat where it's safe!" the yellow fairy urged.

Rose's head turned left, then straight ahead, then right, then left, then right. She was getting dizzy. *Argh!*

"Scram, you guys!" she hissed at the fairies. She waved her arms, batting at the sparkly mist until they disappeared. Then she noticed that a silence had fallen over the Hall.

She grinned weakly at the watching crowd, realizing she must have looked pretty odd, batting at invisible things. Quickly, she scurried back to stand at her place.

Cinda, Snow, Rapunzel, Red, and Pea all gazed at her with concern. "You okay?" asked Cinda.

Avoiding the girls' eyes, Rose mumbled, "Sure. Fine." But really she wanted to dissolve into a puddle under the table. Luckily, the knight-heads called out again, and the announcements continued.

"Attention, students!" they chorused. "There's a second order of business this morning. Your principal needs volunteers to try spinning the legendary treasure — that is, the magical piece of straw that was discovered several weeks ago — into gold. Due to the fact that he has failed miserably at the task himself —"

The principal interrupted them, pounding a fist on the railing. "Dagnabbit! I was going to ask for volunteers myself. And you didn't need to add that last part!"

Turning a more pleasant expression on the students, he spread his arms grandly. "When properly spun, that straw will be the gateway to untold wealth for the Academy, creating lots and lots of gold," he told them. "And all that wealth will protect everyone and everything that the Grimm brothers brought here for safekeeping."

"So the search is on," chorused the helmet-heads, "for that one special person who can spin the straw into gold."

At this second interruption, the principal got really cranky. "Stop it!" he yelled at the helmets. To Rose's surprise he ripped off his hat, and began stomping his feet and jumping around like a crazed cricket. Or more like a three-year-old! Suddenly, he stumbled and toppled from his perch out of sight. *Thonk!*

She gasped with worry, but everyone around her remained surprisingly calm. Did principals act like this all the time? She wouldn't know. This was her first experience with a school, since she'd been tutored at home until now. Behind him, the five helmet-heads rattled and clanked softly on their high wooden shelf. "Calm down. Set a good example for our students," they murmured.

"Oh, shut your visors, you know-it-all can openers!" yelled the principal. Though Rose couldn't see him, she could certainly hear him!

Seeming to think better of his attitude immediately afterward, the principal climbed back up to the balcony railing, apologized to the helmet-heads, and addressed the students again. "There is a box outside in the hallway. Please write your name on a slip of paper and place it in the box. Students will be called out of class one by one in random order to give things a whirl. The spinning of the straw into gold, I mean."

He managed a sunny grin as he surveyed the crowd a final time. "That's all, students. Off to class. And have a happily-ever-after day!"

The musicians blared their trumpets again as the principal left the balcony. And after he was gone, all the students sat to finish eating. Minutes later, the Hickory Dickory Dock clock over in the east balcony end of the Great Hall, spoke up:

"Hickory Dickory Dock,
The mouse ran up the clock.
The clock strikes eight.
First class! Don't be late!
Hickory Dickory Dock."

When the rhyme ended, a mechanical mouse popped out of a little door above the clock's face, which had eyes, a nose, and a mouth. The mouse squeaked cutely eight times to signal the hour. Its squeaks were followed by eight low-toned bongs that echoed throughout the Academy.

Suddenly, dozens of bluebirds that had been flying in the Hall swooped down to the tables. Four of them gathered around each platter, picking them up with their beaks. At the same time, others dipped low in pairs to lift each small silver plate. Then the birds flew off, carrying the dishes behind a curtain in the Hall's serving area. Within seconds, they returned. In their beaks they now carried small silver bowls of water and new white linen napkins, which they set before each student. Like everyone else, Rose dipped her fingers into the bowl she'd been given, and wiped them on the clean napkin.

Afterward as they all stood to go, she realized she didn't know the order of the classes she'd signed up for. Which was her first class of the day? Remembering that Ms. Jabberwocky had put the schedule in her handbook, she picked it up and tried to open it. Only she couldn't seem to pry apart its cover.

Pea nudged her with an elbow and set her own hand-book on the table beside Rose's. Then she pushed the oval on its front. At the same time, she said, "Scrying." Instantly, her book flipped open to a section titled "Scrying."

"Your handbook is like your new best friend when it comes to information," Pea explained. "Just tell it what you want, and it'll fill itself with whatever you request."

"Oh, thanks." Rose pushed the oval on the front of her handbook and said, "Class schedule." Her handbook magically opened itself to the list of classes Ms. Jabberwocky had assigned. Including the two additional classes she'd added to make six.

Grimm Academy Class Assignments for Rose:

Threads

Scrying

Calligraphy and Illuminated Manuscripts

Comportment

Sieges, Catapults, and Jousts

The Grimm History of Barbarians and Dastardlies

"Ooh! Cool!" said Cinda, leaning over to look. "Red and I are in Threads first period, too. C'mon. We'll show you the way to class."

Happily, Rose tucked her handbook in the crook of one arm and followed her new friends.

5

Looking for Loopholes

On the way out of the Hall, the girls passed the sign-up box for spinning straw into gold. Rose knew her parents would have put signing up for such a job on the Danger List if they'd known about it. After all, spindles were sharp spikes used for spinning and twisting fibers.

However the Danger List was gone, thanks to Ms. Jabberwocky's fiery breath, and her parents weren't here to forbid it. Always up for something daring, Rose gleefully put her name in the box, as did her new friends and many other students.

As Rose, Cinda, and Red said farewell to Pea, Snow, and Rapunzel, Rose craned her neck a little, trying to look at Rapunzel's hair without being too obvious about it. Had it grown even longer since yesterday? Now it draped the floor by several inches!

Jousting Boy and some of his friends put their names in after the girls, she noticed, looking back over her shoulder.

As she watched him, she saw a faraway expression come over his face. Suddenly, he stepped to one side of the hallway. Leaning against the wall, he pulled out a little notebook and a pen and began writing. When he glanced up again, he caught her watching him and looked a little embarrassed. Snapping his book shut, he moved on, adopting a tough-guy expression. What was that about? Sometimes, boys could be so grimmzany!

In Threads class, everyone sat where they pleased instead of having assigned seats, so Rose pulled up a chair next to Cinda and Red. The teacher, Ms. Muffet, and her assistant, Ms. Spider, were helping students start crochet projects.

"I'm always losing my sheep, so I think I'll try crocheting a few collars I can string bells on to make it easier to find them," said someone behind them. Rose peered over her shoulder to see a girl with her hair in a ponytail sitting behind her.

A frustrated expression crossed the girl's face just then and she began looking all around herself, checking the floor and her sewing basket. "Oh, *creepers*!" she complained. "I lost my crochet hook! Again. And has anyone seen the yellow yarn?"

"Your hook's tucked behind your ear, Little Bo Peep," Red called. "And I think you might be sitting on your yarn."

"Peepers, thanks!" the ponytail girl called back. Looking delighted to have found both hook and yarn where Red had pointed them out, the girl set to work crocheting collars.

Unlike everyone else in class, Rose only stared at her yarn and hook doubtfully. She figured her parents would approve of crochet. After all, it was done with a blunt hook, not sharp needles. She'd seen her maidservants crochet back at the palace. So she knew there was no chance she might prick her finger or anything. Still . . .

She leaned over and watched as Cinda held her hook in one hand, and fed pink yarn in loops over the hook with her other.

"Having trouble thinking of a project?" Cinda asked her.

Rose nodded. She didn't want to admit that she didn't even know the first thing about crocheting. About any kind of sewing, actually.

"You could make something for your family," Cinda suggested. "I'm making gloves for my dad."

"And I'm making a hat for Wolfgang, a boy in my drama class," said Red "He spends a lot of time in the forest and it can get cold out there."

Rose looked at the drawing Red had made of her idea. The hat she planned had two unusual triangle-shaped peaks on either side of the top.

"Sometimes he shape-shifts," Red explained, seeing her confusion. "Into a real wolf. With wolf ears."

Rose's eyes widened. She'd never met anyone who could shape-shift, much less into a *wolf.* "Oh!" she said. "I see. So those peaks on the hat will fit over his wolf ears. *Good thinking!*"

She watched Red and Cinda work for a few more minutes before finally blurting out, "Here's the thing. I've never done crocheting or any kind of sewing before."

Nearby, there was a gasp and a *thump* sound as Ms. Muffet overheard and fell off her tuffet at this revelation. But then she righted herself on the padded stool behind them. Leaving the student she'd been helping to continue working on her own now, she swung around and patted Rose's hand. "Don't you worry. We'll have you doing all kinds of needlework in no time."

She was right. With a little direction, Rose caught on quickly, and decided to make a scarf for her mom. It started out a little lumpy, with some loose stitches and others too tight. But at least it wasn't unraveling.

And Threads turned out to be lots of fun with Cinda and Red in the class. Time flew by as the three Grimm girls chatted while they worked. Rose found out lots of interesting stuff about her new friends. Like that Cinda had gotten her glass slippers in the library just before a ball, and that

Red's basket had followed her around like a lost puppy until she picked it up. And that Wolfgang was actually Red's crush, and that Cinda had a crush named Prince Awesome.

When they asked if she had a crush, Rose shrugged carelessly, eyes still on her crocheting. "Not really." Because who cared about having a crush? Not her! She had enough to worry about right now. A different *C* word than *Crush* was concerning her. And that word was *Curse*!

"What's your next class?" asked Red when the clock over in the Great Hall bonged the end of the period. The sound was apparently piped through the walls, so everyone could hear it anywhere in the school.

"Scrying," said Rose. "Snow's stepmom teaches that class, right? Her name was in the changed *Rumpel* . . . I mean, in the changed *tale* in the Grimm brothers' room."

"Right. Ms. Wicked," Red said in a neutral tone.

But Cinda appeared worried as the girls stood and put their projects away in workbaskets that would be left in the room till tomorrow. Lowering her voice, she said to Rose, "Remember that certain evil society we were talking about before? Ms. Wicked's a member. So be careful."

Rose's eyes went wide. She nodded, then the girls split up. When she entered the Scrying classroom on the first floor, she took a cautious look around. There were crystal balls of various sizes on shelves, small square mirrors hanging from little silver nails in rows on the far wall, and a glass-fronted cabinet full of strange books.

And there were four melon-size crystal balls magically rolling around atop each of the square tables that filled the room. The students would likely use all those things to try to get a glimpse of events that would happen in the future, she guessed. That was, of course, what scrying was all about!

She asked around until someone pointed her to an unassigned chair at one of the square tables. Once she was seated, a crystal ball rolled her way and parked itself on the table before her. "Uh, hi," she told it. But it didn't reply. Maybe it didn't talk.

Rose set her handbook beside the ball. Since there was no one else at her table yet, and there were still a few minutes before class started, she pushed the oval on the front of her book. "Rules," she instructed it. The book magically opened itself to the very back where she found a list of numbered rules. She ran her finger down them till she got to number 37. It read: "No one is allowed to speak the principal's real name."

"Why not?" she wondered aloud. Suddenly a clear bubble popped out of the book to hover a few inches above the page. *Reason for Rule 37,* it read. *Lest he throw a doozy of a temper tantrum.*

"Oh, thanks," she told the bubble in surprise. Then it popped and disappeared.

So that was the reason you shouldn't say the principal's name aloud! Well, she was glad the other Grimm girls had warned her. If that temper tantrum he'd had during announcements was an example of what could result, she didn't want to stir up his anger. At least he hadn't stayed mad for long before he'd calmed down.

Click! Click! Click! Rose shut her book and glanced up to see the teacher walk into the class, high heels clicking against the floor. Her jaw dropped as the woman drew closer, passing up the aisle. Because Snow's stepmom, Ms. Wicked, was totally, completely gorgeous! Tall, with a heart-shaped face, her black hair was styled high on her head. She wore a large, spiked gold tiara, and carried a stylishly elegant black handbag.

Rose watched her warily as she went to the front of the room. She couldn't stop thinking about Cinda's warning.

Ms. Wicked wrote the day's assignment on a large wall mirror at the front of the class instead of on a chalkboard like Rose's tutors had used back home at the palace. And as she wrote, the teacher would pause now and again to gaze at her reflection in the mirror. Then she would pat her hair in place or straighten her high collar or adjust her necklace or tiara to a more pleasing angle.

Wow, talk about vain! thought Rose. She wondered if Ms. Wicked was going to be able to look away from her own reflection long enough to teach class!

Eventually, though, the teacher directed their attention toward what she'd written. "Today's Assignment: Fairy-Tale Loopholes."

Rose sat up straighter. Huh? This was a weird coincidence. She and the other Grimm girls had just been talking about loopholes as they escaped the library this morning.

"Please select one fairy tale or nursery rhyme of your choice," Ms. Wicked went on. "It can be a tale from the writings of Grimm or any of the other fairy tales or nursery rhymes safeguarded in the Grimmstone Library."

She paused, then went on with an irritated grimace. "Unfortunately, our librarian, Ms. Goose, was unwilling, excuse me, *unable* to lend us the actual fairy-tale and nursery-rhyme books for classroom use. Therefore, you will use your crystal balls to gaze into the tales from afar instead. Please search for anything in the tale or rhyme you select that might be considered a loophole."

A murmur of confusion ran through the class, but then she explained further. "It could be as simple as a word, such as *hole* or *crack* or *opening*. Please note that extra points will be earned if you find unusual loopholes, other than actual words. For instance, anything in the tale or rhyme left unexplained. A story hole if you will. Or an illustration of an object, which contains a net, or some such hole-like thing. This will be an ongoing project, so take your time. Work carefully. Come to me with any questions."

Many of the students chose their own tales for their project. However, not wanting to draw attention to the fact that she and Sleeping Beauty were one and the same person, Rose chose the tale of Rumpelstiltskin instead. When she located it in her crystal ball, she saw that it was the altered tale, not the original one. She looked over at the teacher.

Did she dare point out to her that the tale had been changed? *Yes,* she thought, her wild streak kicking in. Of course she did! She wanted to see how Ms. Wicked would react, so she could report it to the other Grimm girls.

Taking her crystal ball, she went up to the teacher's desk. Up close, she saw that although beautiful, Snow's stepmom's expression was hard and cold.

"Ms. Wicked? I was wondering," she began. "I chose the Rump —" She caught herself just in time. "I mean, Principal R's tale. And I've noticed that it's kind of different now."

Ms. Wicked's eyes narrowed, and she seemed to go on red alert. But her voice was carefully casual when she asked, "Different? How?"

"Well, the principal doesn't spin the straw into gold in the book I found. Not like he did in the original tale," she said. "In fact, in the version I just found *you're* the one who —"

"Oh, no, I think you're mistaken," Ms. Wicked said, smoothly cutting her off. "He never did spin it in his tale. All is as it should be." She looked hard at Rose, her eyes glittering like dark diamonds. "You're new here at the Academy. Briar Rose, correct?"

She nodded. She was going to add, "just call me Rose," when her gaze happened to fall on Ms. Wicked's crystal ball. It was sitting on the teacher's desk, and the title of the fairy tale she'd been reading was — *Sleeping Beauty*! Now it was Rose's turn to go on red alert. This was certainly a worrisome coincidence, but she didn't know quite what to make of it.

"Well, mistakes happen," the teacher said dismissively. "But good job. You may be seated now."

After that, every time Rose looked up from her desk, the teacher seemed to be watching her. Luckily, there were several versions of her story, and the one in the teacher's crystal ball wasn't one that used her actual "Briar Rose" name. So maybe she was safe from discovery. She hoped so, anyway.

As class ended, Ms. Wicked called her up to her desk before she could leave for third-period Calligraphy. "It's so nice to have you in my class," she told Rose with a pleasant and disarming smile. "Your work today with the crystal ball was exemplary, especially since I assume it was your first time scrying?"

Rose nodded.

"Well, since you show such . . . talent, perhaps I'll excuse you from homework this semester so that you can help me with a certain . . . special project. We'll discuss this further another time. That will be all for now."

"Oh, okay. Thanks," said Rose. Why, Ms. Wicked was kind of nice! Not cold and hard as she'd first thought, and not at all like the other Grimm girls had described her. Rose left the class feeling a bit confused, but pleased.

Her third-period Calligraphy and Illuminated Manuscripts class was taught by Sir Peter Pen. He wore a green vest, green pants, and green hat, along with a white shirt and brown boots. And he moved around the classroom in leaps, sailing through the air as if on an invisible trampoline as he went to help students. Their assignment was to practice flourishes, which were embellishments added to handwritten letters of the alphabet to add beauty and visual excitement. Starting with an italic lettering style called Copperplate, she and her classmates used their pens to add swoops, curlicues, and swirls.

As they practiced hand lettering, Rose couldn't help but remember the magic pen from the Grimm brothers' room that morning. Too bad she didn't have it now. Calligraphy would be a snap!

Later, at lunch, she told the other Grimm girls what had happened in Scrying, and they seemed suspicious about what Ms. Wicked was having Rose's class do. Red and Snow took Scrying, too, but not till the afternoon, so they'd had no idea that Ms. Wicked was asking her classes to look for loopholes.

"She's up to something," Red said, to which Cinda and Rapunzel nodded.

Snow sighed. "No doubt you're right."

Pea arrived just then and announced, "My name was pulled from the spin-the-straw box, so I went to this little room high in the library. Ms. Goose told me how to find it. You go through a door in Section *S* marked *Spinning* and then up a million or so winding stairs to a room where the spindle is. Anyway, so I went there and tried to spin that dumb straw into gold."

"I'm guessing it didn't go so well?" said Rose.

Pea rolled her eyes. "That's an understatement. If you ask me, the principal is grasping at straws thinking anyone will ever be able to spin that straw into gold. They won't."

"Why?" asked Rapunzel.

"Because it doesn't want to be spun. Every time I tried, it jumped out of my hands like some kind of loony wiggle worm."

Her description started the Grimm girls laughing.

"I guess it *was* kind of funny," Pea admitted, smiling, too. "But, seriously, I spent the whole time chasing it down. And I was super nervous because Principal Rumpus was majorly antsy while I was doing it — or *trying* to do it, anyway."

Rose was still smiling to herself about Pea's funny story as the two of them went to fourth-period Comportment class on the second floor, which they'd discovered they had together. Rose's palace tutors had schooled her in Comportment for years, so she already knew it was basically a class about manners. No biggie. This would be a cinch. As they entered the classroom, she saw a long table draped in linen. At one end were stacks of fancy plates, silverware, glasses, and napkins. The room was decorated with balloons and streamers as if they were going to have a party.

The teacher's name was written across the board on the front wall: Ms. Queenharts of Wonderland. Fittingly, her dress was covered with white, pink, and red hearts, and she wore a small red crown. As the girls crossed the room, they watched the teacher set three trays of cupcakes on the table, spacing them out down the center of it.

"Mmm, cupcakes," Rose remarked to Pea as they found desks next to each other behind the long linen-draped table. "I have a feeling I'm going to like this class!"

Both girls giggled.

Noticing their laughter, Ms. Queenharts aimed her laser-beam eyes in Rose's direction. "Something amusing you, young lady? Maybe you'd like to tell the whole class?"

"Um, no, thank you," said Rose.

"Well, one more outburst of giggles from either of you ladies, and it'll be off with your heads! Off with your heads!"

Rose's eyes widened and her mouth formed a surprised *O*. Because this teacher was kind of hilarious. Though she probably didn't mean to be, she was so over-the-top, it was funny. Rose couldn't help giggling again. So it was a good thing for her that Ms. Queenharts had switched her attention to some other student and didn't notice this time.

"Today we will study the art of invitation etiquette, party planning and manners, and place settings," Ms. Queenharts announced after the period began.

Most of the class time was spent learning the proper way to set places for a large dinner party. Rose already knew where the various pieces of silverware went, even the unusual ones like grapefruit spoons and shrimp forks. As a princess, she'd eaten many fancy meals over the years.

It was late in the period when they finally moved on to the other parts of the lesson. By now Rose was having a hard time trying not to yawn. She never felt well rested after a night of sleepwalking. But yawning during a lesson in manners seemed like a bad idea, so she tried her best not to.

Suddenly, Ms. Queenharts said something that jolted her wide-awake. "You all know the tale of Sleeping Beauty."

Rose stiffened in her chair. *Oh, grindlesnorts!* Had this teacher guessed who she really was? She didn't seem to be singling her out, though.

Ms. Queenharts went on. "We will use this particular fairy tale as an example of the consequences of bad manners." She gestured toward the table at the front of the room, which they had set during the earlier place-setting lesson. "Now, how many golden plates do you see?"

"Twelve," everyone answered.

"Correct. The reason for the curse put upon Sleeping Beauty was that her family only invited twelve of the thirteen fairies in their village to the party celebrating their daughter's birth. The thirteenth fairy was understandably upset. No one enjoys being left out. Assuming there had been some mistake, she went to the party, anyway. She was even thoughtful enough to take a gift, which she bestowed on the newborn child, despite her justifiable anger."

What? Speaking of anger, Ms. Queenharts's twisting of her tale was making Rose steaming mad. The teacher had slanted the tale to make her family look bad. Well, she wouldn't let her get away with that!

"That's not fair!" she blurted, jumping up. "My — um, that is, *Sleeping Beauty's* — family owned no more than twelve golden plates. That's the reason they only invited twelve fairies. Besides that, the thirteenth fairy was well-known to be grumpy and unkind. And her gift to Sleeping Beauty was a curse! Talk about bad manners!"

"We'll study mannerly and unmannerly curses later this year," Ms. Queenharts replied with surprising calm. Her own manners were far milder now that she was engrossed in teaching. "But perhaps we can touch on the subject now," she mused. "Is it ever acceptable to answer bad manners from someone else with bad manners of your own?" Her gaze scanned the students, a brow arched in question.

In answer, some students voted yes and others no. Again, Rose couldn't stop herself from speaking up. "But the thirteenth fairy's curse was worse than bad manners, remember? It foretold that sometime after Sleeping Beauty turned twelve, she would prick her finger on a sharp object and *die*!"

"That does seem way worse than just bad manners," Pea agreed softly.

Rose sent her a grateful look before going on. "Luckily the twelfth fairy had not yet given her gift. So after the thirteenth fairy uttered that horrible curse, fairy number twelve softened the curse so that Sleeping Beauty would only *fall asleep* for one hundred years. Sure, that thirteenth fairy was slighted by my father, but —"

"*Your* father?" interrupted Ms. Queenharts. She pointed a finger at her. (Which was, of course, rude in itself, thought Rose.) "You! Why, you're Sleeping Beauty, aren't you?" the teacher guessed. "Of course you are! Rose. Briar Rose. Sleeping Beauty. All one and the same. I didn't make the connection when you were first introduced this morning."

Everyone gasped and heads swiveled to stare at Rose. Suddenly realizing what she'd let slip, she toyed with the quill pen on her desk, gripping it hard as people began to whisper. *Her birthday is coming up, isn't it? We'd better be careful around her. Wouldn't want her to get an injury and fall asleep for a hundred years.*

"Want me to hold your pen for you?" Pea offered gently. "So you don't accidentally, um . . . you know . . . prick your finger?"

Aghhh! Rose wanted to scream and cry and run away all at the same time. How grimmorrible! And her first day here had been going so well! But now she'd let the cat out of the bag and everyone was going all overprotective on her. Just as she'd feared would happen if anyone knew!

6

Joust Between Friends

Rose slumped in her seat. "No, you don't need to hold my pen, but thanks, anyway," she told Pea. "I don't have to be careful till Friday. I'm not twelve . . . yet."

"Indeed, Sleeping Beauty's father may not have meant to be unkind. And perhaps he didn't intend to behave in an unmannerly way," Ms. Queenharts admitted to the class, drawing their attention away from Rose at last. "However, the thirteenth fairy should never have been left out simply for lack of an additional gold plate. She could have been given another plate — perhaps a silver one."

Rose couldn't argue with that. But really, who wanted to invite a grumpy fairy to a party? She could see that the fairy's feelings might have been hurt. However, she'd way overreacted with that curse. And, in doing so, she'd pretty much changed Rose's life forever. All because of hurt feelings.

Luckily, the school clock began to bong just then. Rose grabbed her handbook, jumped up, and fled the room. She was so eager to escape, she even forgot to say bye to Pea. She just wanted to get out of there as fast as possible. But where could she go to get away from everyone? And away from the truth. That she was *cursed*.

Feeling desperate, she dashed downstairs and outside. She would go find Starlight and . . . and, what? She paused uncertainly as she reached the garden. Because there was really nowhere she could go to escape her curse. It would find her no matter where she went!

If only she could somehow have one last great, amazing adventure before her birthday this Friday, though. Something she could remember forever. Even after she turned into a twelve-year-old wimpette who had to steer clear of anything remotely resembling fun in order to avoid a one-hundred-year nap. But what could that adventure be? She didn't have much time.

Clank. Clank. Clank. What was that? Rose stepped from the garden onto the lawn and peered toward the sounds. Directly across Once Upon River on the lawn next to Gray Castle, she could see a bunch of students wearing armor. Most were boys, but there were a few girls, too.

Apparently, she'd just found her fifth-period Sieges, Catapults, and Jousts class by accident. One problem, however: She'd need to get across the river to attend it.

Just then, a student walked past her. It was Jousting Boy! He glanced back at her, then stopped. "Lost again?"

"Again? Oh, you mean like in the library this morning. Yeah, well, at least I'm not in my pj's this time, right?" She managed a smile, and he smiled, too. "Really, I don't know why I brought that up. Believe me, I'd rather forget about it. I have enough problems right now."

"Anything I can do?" he asked. When she shook her head, he seemed to take her at her word. With a wave good-bye, he headed down to the river's edge, where he untethered a swan-shaped boat.

"Wait! Are you crossing the river?" she called.

When he nodded, she jogged to his side and climbed aboard. Only then did she ask, "Mind taking a passenger?"

"Sure, but . . ." He looked around them uncertainly. ". . . to where?"

Rose pointed to the opposite side of the river, where a man who had lots of muscles and wore a whistle around his neck was walking among the students on the lawn. They'd broken into groups now. Some were working with jousting poles, others were launching various objects high into the air using catapults. A third group seemed to be planning an attack on the castle, for class practice.

"You want to talk to the coach? Does that mean you're

taking SCJ? Sieges, Catapults, and Jousts class?" he asked, tossing the rope that had tethered the boat inside it.

When she nodded, he climbed into the boat with his jousting pole, still looking surprised at the idea, though she wasn't sure why he should be. After all, there were several other girls in the class over on the lawn.

"Got a problem with that?" Rose asked super-sweetly. Learning to joust back home hadn't been easy for her, given how overprotective her parents had always been. However, she'd managed to get some of the palace guards to teach her the basics. And she'd sworn them to secrecy not to tell her parents about her love of the sport.

"Nope," he replied. "It's just that when I was back in the hall a minute ago I heard someone say that you're actually Sleeping Beauty?"

She stiffened. News about her identity had sure traveled fast. "Uh-huh. So?"

"So jousting poles aren't all that sharp, but still. Pointy poles . . . your fairy-tale curse. Doesn't seem like the two mix. Get my point?" The prince touched the tip of his jousting pole as if to demonstrate, then smiled at his joke.

She scowled at him. "That's my business," she said rather hotly. "Besides, the curse in my fairy tale doesn't kick in until my birthday on Friday. Till then, I don't have to worry. And I'm good at jousting. So look out!"

"Whoa! Okay, I will," he said chuckling at her determination. He lay his jousting pole in the bottom of the boat and then picked up the oars and paddled them across. "It'll be awesome to have you in class, actually. We could use some new, good competition."

When they reached the Gray Castle side of the river, he picked up his pole, jumped out of the boat, and then offered her a hand up. She took it, which was only proper princess manners, after all.

As soon as she was on land again he gave her a grin over his shoulder. "Good luck, jouster," he told her, then he jogged off ahead. She grinned, too, and followed, feeling her spirits lift a little at his easygoing attitude.

"Coach?" she said, going up to the teacher, who had his back to her. In response, the coach leaped around, muscles tense, looking like he expected trouble.

Grimmness! Was he always this jumpy?

Seeing nothing amiss, he relaxed and greeted her calmly. After Rose explained she was to be in his class, she hurriedly added, "I'm most interested in learning the skills of a knight, like jousting and swordplay."

"Then suit up. Ask one of the other girls for some help," he instructed her, pointing toward a pile of armor.

"No help needed. I've worn armor before," she called as she dashed off in the direction he'd pointed. And she had worn it — once. When she was seven years old, she'd taken down one of the suits of armor standing in the halls of the palace back home and put it all on, piece by piece. The armor had dwarfed her small body and been impossible to walk in. She'd wound up sprawled on her back with her arms and legs in the air, unable to flip herself over, like some kind of strange beetle. Plus, for all her trouble, she'd gotten a terrible scolding about sharp edges and such. But she wasn't going to tell the coach that.

Rose hurriedly suited up, draping plate armor over her dress, until she was covered in metal from the top of her head (helm) to the super-short skirt (tasset) that flared out from her waist. Luckily, this armor actually fit her! By the time she was ready, the coach was already standing before the jousters and had started to give a short introduction. She clanked over to join them. She was so excited to be in a real knight class!

"Although lances may be used while mounted on horseback, today we will practice without mounts," the coach told them. "Now, remember, a jousting lance's tip is blunt. This will unseat your opponent from his horse rather than spear him and cause deadly harm. The shafts of our lances are hollow so that they will break on impact. Yet another safeguard. However, should you accidentally impale your opponent, it's an automatic F in this class and expulsion from the Academy. Not to mention horrible. So no blood-shed! Got it?"

"Got it!" the students shouted back in unison. Rose was a little disappointed. Was this class all going to be about safety? She wanted to get to the good part where they'd do some swordplay or something daring.

Just then, one of the other student groups launched a large boulder from a catapult some distance away. When it landed off-target in the river with a huge splash, the racket sent the coach jumping a foot high. He stared toward the kids who'd misfired, his eyes bugging out.

But then, after taking a few deep breaths to calm himself, he turned back to Rose's group again. "All right, jousters!" he said, punching an energetic fist in the air. "Get moving! And remember. Safety first. I'll check back in a few minutes."

Before Rose could shut her visor, one of the boy jousters spoke to her. "Wait! Is it true? Are you Sleeping Beauty?"

Drat. Recognized again! She nodded before quickly flipping down her visor. Still cross at herself for letting the cat out of the bag about her identity — and for letting Ms. Queenharts get under her skin — she played badly against all her opponents. Which were really just hay bales. The coach wasn't taking any chances letting them joust with each other yet.

The tall stacks of square hay bales were each hung with full-size pictures of menacing knights. Students ran and aimed their poles at the pictures. Though Rose was normally very coordinated, every move she made was off-balance today. She missed target after target, and almost broke her lance once.

After a particularly clumsy thrust, she got frustrated and flipped up her visor. "C'mon. Just because I'm Sleeping Beauty doesn't mean you should go easy on me!" she jokingly scolded the paper knight on her hay bale stack.

Seeing some of the guys nearby staring, she swung around to face them. They had all been giving her a wide berth whenever they charged a target, waiting to make sure she was well out of their way before they ran. They were acting like she was made of fragile glass. It was annoying!

Now she pointedly touched the end of her jousting pole with her fingers as they watched. "See?" she told them. "I touched something sort of sharp and didn't crumple to the ground and start a hundred-year deep sleep or anything. So stop acting so proper around me, and act more . . . knightly, okay?"

"You mean like him?" one of the boys asked in a laughing tone. He cocked the thumb of his steel-gloved hand toward another student.

When the guy he'd pointed at raised his visor, Rose saw it was Jousting Boy, the one who'd rowed her over here. His lips curved in a slight smile, showing a hint of white teeth. The other students were grinning, too. She didn't get it.

"What's so funny?" she demanded, wondering if they might be making fun of her.

"You said 'knightly,'" Jousting Boy informed her, coming over. "And that's my name. Knightly."

"It is? And you want to be a knight?" A giggle escaped her.

"I know, I know," he said good-naturedly. "For a long time I was confused as to why my parents always repeated my name three times right before I went to sleep. But they were actually saying, 'Nighty night, Knightly.'"

She giggled again.

"Okay, no more special treatment," he promised her. "Right, guys?" he said, looking around at the other students. They nodded, going back to their practice.

"One thing, though." Knightly adjusted the lance she held to a different angle for her. "There. You'll probably have more luck with it in that position."

"Thanks," she told him gratefully. He'd obviously guessed she didn't have much training. They got back into jousting stance again. Her confidence somewhat restored, Rose charged her target again and again, making a series of strikes that had some students applauding her with new respect. She was pretty surprised at how well she'd done, too!

"Good job!" Knightly called out to her when class was over.

"You, too," she called back, for she'd sneaked peeks now and then and knew he was skilled. She headed over to the equipment area where she'd gotten her armor.

"If Knightly's giving you pointers, he must think you're good. He's the best on the jousting team and can spot raw talent," one of the girl jousters murmured to her as they took off their armor. When the girl removed her helmet, Rose saw it was Little Bo Peep from Threads class. "He wins the tournament every year," the girl went on.

"Uh, thanks for telling me," Rose said. She liked that Knightly hadn't boasted about himself to her.

Little Bo Peep's brow knit and she glanced around, that familiar confused expression crossing her face. "Oh, peepers, has anybody seen my blue slipper?" she called to the students who were getting unsuited nearby. When someone called out that they'd spotted it, the girl took off toward them just as Knightly came over to Rose. He'd taken off all of his armor except his helmet. Removing it now, he placed it in the box with the rest of the class helmets.

"Can't believe it's sixth period already. What's your last class of the day?" he asked Rose.

"History," she told him as she started to leave. Behind them, she could hear Little Bo Peep asking around about her handbook now. She'd apparently lost that, too.

"Want me to walk you?" Knightly offered, falling into step with Rose.

"Thanks, that'll help," she replied. "Because, honestly, I have no idea how to get to the classroom from this side of the school. Is it on your way?"

"No. But it's the code of the knights to help anyone in distress. And since you're new and might get lost, I'm avoiding the possibility of distress before it happens. Okay?"

He grinned and she laughed, saying, "Sure."

Together, they walked across the lawn in silence, before crossing the drawbridge and entering Gray Castle. "Your parents must be really proud of your skill. You'll make a fine knight someday," she told him as she studied the halls in the boys' side of the school. Here, the walls were a pale gray marble, but the columns and layout looked pretty much the same as the girls' side.

The walls were hung with lavish tapestries showing

scenes of feasts and pageantry. And there were flowers, birds, and gargoyles carved at the top of the hall's tall, stone support columns. It all reminded her of home, for she'd grown up in a palace almost as beautiful, though much smaller than the Academy.

He shrugged in response to her question. "I guess."

"You don't sound very excited," she said in surprise. "But how can you not be? I'd jump at the chance to become a knight if only I could."

"Mostly I'm doing what my parents expect. See, I come from a long line of knights. My two older brothers are jousting grand-prize medalists in the annual Grimmlandia tournaments." He shot her a quick look, then paused to open the door to the Great Hall for her so they could cross through it over to Pink Castle. "Guess what their names are?"

She pretended to think hard. "Sorry," she said after a few seconds. "I give up."

"Prince Midknight and Prince Goodknight." He spelled the names out for her.

She laughed as they entered the girls' hall. "Seriously?"

He nodded, grinning, too. "Dead serious."

"You and your brothers are lucky to have parents who support your dream," she said.

He sent her a strange look, then said something that sounded like, "Yeah, I wish." Then he added, "Why are you so interested in knighthood?"

"I've wanted to be a knight, like, forever," she confided. "But my parents vetoed that idea. Not because they don't think I'm capable of becoming one. They know girls can do anything boys can. No, it's because of that stupid curse in my fairy tale. I've heard objections like this all my life: *'Knights can find themselves in all sorts of peril involving sharp objects. Blah, blah, blah.'*"

That curse had always stood between her and what she wanted. Still, she felt pretty happy right at the moment. She'd gotten some jousting practice, and now this nice boy was walking her to class. Plus, she'd made lots of other friends already at GA.

"Don't give up," Knightly told her, as they paused together in the hall. "If you really want to learn everything there is to know about knighthood, Coach is the best. And if you need any pointers or have any questions, I'll help you anytime."

"Really? Thanks!"

He nodded, then pointed at the classroom door behind her. "Well, this is History," he told her. "And now I'm history!" So saying, he flashed a grin and loped off back the way they'd come. But after just a few steps, he looked back at her and called, "See you!"

Rose smiled and sent him a wave, then he was quickly swallowed up by the crowd of students moving through the hall. "Bye," she murmured softly, even though he was too far away to hear by now. With a small smile still curving her lips, she turned and entered the classroom.

7
Eggsactly

Once inside the Grimm History of Barbarians and Dastardlies classroom, Rose was surprised to see an enormous egg walking around. Turned out, he was the teacher. He was about a foot taller than she was, with skinny legs that ended in very pointy shoes, which were twice as long as normal-size feet.

When the egg stepped toward her, she noticed that his shell was cracked in a few places. And that he wore an orange tunic and held a snazzy walking stick that he tapped on the floor now and then.

He smiled at her in welcome, causing the faint cracks in his cheeks to show a little more. "And eggsactly who might you be?" he asked.

"Rose. I'm new." She curtsied prettily. Her tutors at the palace had spent hours teaching her the art of various curtsies. So she knew just the right way to do it when meeting a person of authority.

"I'm Mr. Hump-Dumpty. With a hyphen," the egg-teacher informed her. He waved his walking stick toward the rows of chairs in the room. "Take any seat. They're not assigned."

As Rose scanned the room, Bo Peep waved her over. Glad to see someone she knew, Rose went and sat behind her.

"Looks like we have three classes together," Little Bo Peep said to her. "You're Rose, right?" When Rose nodded, Bo Peep asked, "Do you see my folder of homework peep-ers, I mean papers, by any chance? I had them two seconds ago out in the hall, but I now I can't find them." She leaned over to check under her chair.

"No, sorry," Rose said, after also looking around. This girl seemed to have a real problem keeping track of her belongings.

Bo Peep sighed, then grinned. "That's okay. I think maybe I left them in my trunker after all."

Both girls turned to face front as the teacher spoke up. "Today we will study the Wall," Mr. Hump-Dumpty announced. "As you all know, Grimmlandia includes the Wall, the Academy, Once Upon River, the outlying vil-lages, and —"

He swung about suddenly and pointed the tip of his walking stick at Bo Peep. "And Neverwood Forest," she answered easily. "So called because you 'never would' venture into that forest. Not if you had half a brain, anyway."

"Correggt!" Mr. Hump-Dumpty praised her. He continued circling the room. "And what separates Grimmlandia from the Barbarians and Dastardlies?"

He swiveled suddenly to point his walking stick at Red Riding Hood. Rose hadn't even noticed she was in the class till just now.

"The Wall. And beyond that is the Dark Nothingterror," Red supplied. Catching Rose's eye, she sent her a tiny wave, and Rose waved back.

"Eggsellent!" said Mr. Hump-Dumpty. "What an eggsceptional group of students you are!"

Now his walking stick whipped around, and he pointed to Rose. "And what is the Dark Nothingterror?"

"It's where the Barbarians and Dastardlies hang out," she answered. You didn't need to learn that in school. Everyone in Grimmlandia already knew it. However, the casual way she said it made a few students giggle.

"Perfeggt! Now let's talk more about them and the eggstreme danger they represent." Mr. Hump-Dumpty's expression went seriously serious as he began going on and on about the dangers of Neverwood Forest, the Wall, and the mythical creatures beyond it. He would definitely get along with that pesky yellow fairy in the mist that appeared to her now and then, thought Rose. Because he was a huge worrywart!

After a while, some students got restless during his lecture, and started passing notes or doodling on vellum. They'd probably heard these cautions and descriptions many times before. However, Rose listened closely and took notes. She was fascinated.

What an eggsciting, um, exciting thing it would be to ride to the Wall and back on Starlight, she thought. Did she dare eggscape, er, escape for a little while to make the journey?

She'd have to travel through Neverwood Forest, though. And Bo Peep had said no one would venture there if they had half a brain. Rose did have a brain, and she liked to think it was a whole one. Maybe she could use it to keep her and her unicorn safe from harm on such a trip. She couldn't think of anything more delightfully daring than going to see the Wall, a mysterious, legendary, dangerous place. It would be the very adventure she'd longed to have before her birthday brought that curse down on her head. The perfect, most grimmtabulous adventure of her life!

Her hand shot in the air as enthusiasm for the idea swelled within her. "What's the Wall made of?"

"Magic," Mr. Hump-Dumpty replied rather unhelpfully.

"Has anyone ever seen it?" she prodded him.

Unfortunately, this question sent Mr. Hump-Dumpty into a fearful tizzy. He fixed the entire class with his big, worried egg eyeballs. "One must absolutely never, ever venture close enough to look upon the Wall. For if someone were to go there, dare to sit on the Wall, and then have a great fall from it, there would be a fifty-fifty chance they'd tip out of Grimmlandia and into the Dark Nothingterror. And then all the king's horses and all the king's men could not put that someone together again!"

This warning was followed at length by others, but Rose missed the rest of his lecture because she started to nod off — along with probably half the class. When the Hickory Dickory clock bonged, she jerked awake. She'd been having a dream that she was on a ride to the Wall with the wind in her hair. Just Starlight and her cruising through the forest. The smell of trees and flowers, the cool shade, and the fresh air had been so vivid. It had seemed so real. So magical. So possible. So grimmtastic! An excited hope filled her.

And a little weariness, too. It was pure luck that she hadn't gone sleepwalking or started snoring in the middle of class, she decided as she stood to go. Now that school was over for the day, she was really exhausted. She barely made it through dinner before she bid the others at her table a sleepy good night.

The next morning, Rose woke up in bed. *Score!* She hadn't gone sleepwalking again. In a jiff, she was off to breakfast.

It didn't take long for her good mood to dim, however. As she walked down the hall, she couldn't help noticing that whispers followed her. Students she hadn't even met were staring when they didn't think she saw. Was it because they'd all heard she was Sleeping Beauty?

At breakfast in the Great Hall, Snow and her three Grimm girlfriends acted stiff with her, like she'd done something to offend them. Conversation among them was awkward, mostly things like "pass the salt" and "these knick-knack paddy-whack pancakes are delish." And when a boy came over that Rose figured must be Wolfgang, Red didn't even introduce him to her.

Why were they acting so distant? She'd done nothing wrong! Feeling out of sorts now, Rose stomped off to first period, ahead of Red and Cinda.

Yesterday, it had been such fun chatting with those two girls during Threads class. But today they barely spoke to her as they worked on their crochet projects. They didn't exactly *ignore* her. They were polite as ever, just not as friendly as before. Something was definitely up.

"Are you mad at me for some reason?" Rose asked them at last, stilling the movement of her crochet hook. Ms. Spider and Ms. Muffet were on the other side of the room, so it felt "safe" to chat freely about matters other than needlework. "Or maybe you think you need to whisper around me and be overly careful now that you know Rose equals Sleeping Beauty? But, look. That's not a problem. Honest. It's three days till I turn twelve. And who knows? Maybe the curse won't come true, and I'll be able to totally avoid the longest nap ever."

They smiled at her little joke, but didn't laugh. "We understand," Cinda said mildly, but Red looked away, busying herself with something inside her basket.

Rose sighed, not understanding. What had changed since yesterday?

In second and third periods, things went pretty much the same. Students seemed to be avoiding her. No one talked to her or sat by her. She felt unwelcome. Like she was being punished for something she didn't do.

By contrast, Ms. Wicked was super nice to her in Scrying. "I have a feeling you and I are going to become good friends," she gushed to Rose. And instead of having her look for loopholes in fairy tales like the rest of the class, Ms. Wicked sent her on an errand to buy some mirror polish from the school store. Last thing she needed was to become an evil teacher's pet!

Still, Rose went on the errand. What else could she do?

The Academy store was called The Cupboard, and it was tucked away on the fourth floor.

When she got there she saw that the door to the store was the kind where the top half opened separately from the bottom half. Right now, the top half of the door was open, probably so students could speak to the shopkeeper, who could then duck back inside to get whatever they needed. Rose stuck her head in. Immediately, a little dog in the shop started barking. It was small as a puppy, and totally adorable, all white except for a black circle around one eye and a corkscrew tail.

"Hellooo!" an elderly woman greeted her briskly from inside the little store. "I'm glad you've come."

She was? How strange, thought Rose. The woman acted like she'd been expecting her!

"I'm Mother Hubbard," the shopkeeper went on, swinging open the bottom half of the door so that Rose could walk through. "And this is Prince Puppy," she added, gesturing toward her dog. Then for some reason she stepped out of the store into the hall, shutting the bottom half of the door behind herself. Meanwhile, her dog jumped all around. Suddenly, it leaped high into Rose's arms.

"Whoa! You sure have a lot of energy, Prince," Rose told him, laughing as he tried to lick her chin.

She looked up again to see that Mother Hubbard had started off down the hall. "Wait! Where are you going? I need to buy something. And what about your dog?" Rose called after her.

At the mention of her dog, Mother Hubbard paused and clutched her hands together below her chin, gazing back at the dog with an adoring expression on her face. Her eyes shifted to Rose, and she abruptly began speaking in rhyme:

> *"That wonderful dog*
> *is my delight.*
> *Until I return,*
> *do keep him in sight.*
> *While I'm off to the hatter's*
> *To buy him a hat,*
> *Just remember one thing:*
> *Keep him far from the cat!"*

She snapped her fingers, then clicked her heels. And just like that, Mother Hubbard was gone. She hadn't walked away. She'd just disappeared right in the middle of the hall.

"What was that all about?" Rose wondered aloud. Mother Hubbard might be magical, but she also acted a bit batty. Since when did a dog need a hat, anyway? Now that she was gone, Rose looked around, unsure what to do. Should she go back to class, or . . .

She glanced around the store. It was smaller than her dorm room. There was a little desk with a chair off to one side. Aside from that, all four walls were covered with dozens of doors, each of a different size and shape, and each with a different sort of doorknob.

She glanced at the dog. "Mind if I look around? My teacher wants some polish for her mirrors."

Of course she hadn't expected a reply. But when she put the dog down, it immediately ran to a door set low in the wall and pawed at it. Hope rose in her. "Is that where the polish is?" Maybe she wouldn't have to go back to Ms. Wicked empty-handed after all.

Kneeling, she saw that the door the dog was sniffing around was cut in the shape of a cat silhouette. An irritated-looking cat with an arching back. Was there actually a cat sleeping inside?

"Let's not open that one, okay?" Rose murmured, remembering what Mother Hubbard had said about keeping this dog far from the cat. She wasn't taking any chances. The pooch let out a disappointed-sounding snort, then trotted over and curled up in his basket to nap.

Rose stood and began opening more doors along the wall, one after the other, hoping she'd luck into finding the polish.

Some of the doors were so teeny-tiny that the cabinets they opened to held only one spool of thread or an eraser. Others doors were tall and skinny and held things like fishing rods or baseball bats. One door was round, with a single beach ball inside. There were even star-shaped and diamond-shaped doors. Who could guess what was behind them? Not her! But the really unusual thing about all these doors was that they constantly resized themselves after being opened and shut, so that the cabinets then contained something completely different than before. Weird!

"Hello?" said a voice. Rose looked over to see a girl with turquoise hair standing at the store entrance. It was Mermily, the girl she'd seen splashing around in the fifth-floor fountain that first night with Pea. The bottom half of the store's door was closed now, so Rose couldn't see below her waist. Unfortunately. Because she was dying to know if the girl still had a fishtail!

"Hi," said Rose.

Mermily returned her greeting, not seeming to remember her. And maybe that was a good thing. If this mermaid-girl recognized her, would she start treating her stiffly like the other Grimm girls?

"Do you have any turquoise rubber boots?" asked Mermily. She stuck her head in the door to glance around. "Where's Mother Hubbard?"

"She's gone," said Rose.

Mermily looked so disappointed that Rose added, "But I'll see what I can find. Just a sec." She dashed over and began checking doors big enough to possibly hold boots. But when she got there, each cupboard was bare. Weird!

"Um, I can't seem to find any boots," she told Mermily after a few minutes of searching. The girl looked really disappointed at this news, but what could Rose do?

"Okay, I'll come back later," said Mermily. As she headed off, Rose leaned out of the top half of the store door to watch. That answered that question. No tail. Of course, she had been asking for boots, and why would you need those if you didn't have feet? She could obviously shape-shift between mermaid and not. Like Red had said, Wolfgang could shift between a four-legged wolf and a regular two-legged person.

Rose sighed, then looked at the dog. "I don't suppose you could take care of yourself if I leave?" The dog raised his head from his basket, and sent her a sad look, as if he had understood what she'd said and didn't want her to go.

"Okay, okay," she said. "I'll stay. But only till the end of second period." If Mother Hubbard wasn't back by then, she'd take the dog to the office and ask Ms. Jabberwocky to look after him, she decided.

Thump! Thump! The dog wagged his corkscrew tail. Then he leaped from his basket and dashed over to one of the cupboards Rose hadn't yet tried. He pawed at it.

She raised a suspicious brow. "I hope that's not another cat door." When he started acting even more excited, she said, "Okay, then. If you promise me it's not a cat door, I'll open it."

"Woof!" he replied, wagging his tail even faster.

Hoping for mirror polish, she went to the wall and opened the door. Instead, she found rubber boots in the cabinet. Cute, shiny turquoise ones like Mermily had wanted. But when Rose went and leaned out of the top half of the door to call her back, the hall was empty.

"Oh, how vexing!" she murmured. As she replaced the boots in the cabinet, she said to the dog, "Are you sure you don't know where the mirror polish is?"

In response, the dog dashed over to a new wall door and began pawing at it. This one was as tall and wide as she was. Too tall and wide to hold just a bottle of mirror polish, she thought with disappointment. However, when she opened it, that was exactly what she found. There were five shelves, with a single bottle of mirror polish sitting on the topmost one.

"Good boy," Rose praised. The dog wagged his tail and actually grinned.

She reached into the cupboard. However, when she tried to clutch the bottle, she caught only air. And when her fingers brushed the back wall of the cupboard . . . they went through it! She drew back, gasping in surprise. After a few stunned seconds, she looked down at the dog. "I don't suppose you can explain that?"

Grinning mischievously now, he simply trotted over to his bed under the desk and curled up to nap again. Rose tried once more to grab the polish. This time, her hand and arm went through the rear of the cupboard up to her elbow! Quickly, she yanked her arm back, then stared at her hand. Instead of polish, she'd grabbed a fistful of green leaves. She stared uncertainly into the cupboard. Was there some kind of garden behind it? Or what?

Did she dare find out? She did! Before she could consider the dangers of what she was about to do, that daredevil side of her rose up to urge her on. This could be her only chance for one last amazing adventure before Friday.

Without another thought, she leaped through the back of the cupboard! For a few moments everything became a blur of fuzzy kaleidoscope colors as she was whisked away to wherever the cupboard had decided to take her.

Thump! On the other side, she fell through a green hedge and landed on her back upon soft grass.

Hearing loud, fierce grinding noises, she sat up and stared around warily. Before her, not ten feet ahead, stood a wall. An impossibly tall one that seemed to rise as high as the clouds. She looked left but couldn't see where it ended in the far distance. She looked right. Same thing.

Her breath caught, and she scrambled backward on her bent elbows as she realized something. She must have magically arrived at the borders of the realm — at the very edge of Grimmlandia!

And this wasn't just any old wall. It was *the* Wall. The one Mr. Hump-Dumpty warned everyone about in History class. The infamous one that surrounded the realm. The one no one had ever visited as far as she knew. It was thick and appeared to be made of slippery frosted glass.

When Rose leaped to her feet, she noticed something floating high overhead. It looked like a long, winding stream of black ants. It had come from the distance behind her and was moving out of Grimmlandia, over the Wall into the Nothingterror. As it did, the grinding, crunching, slurping, smacking sounds on the other side of the Wall grew briefly louder. She put her hands over her ears to muffle the horrible sounds.

A few seconds later, another string of ants rose from the Nothingterror side of the Wall and flew high overhead back toward the Academy! Who had sent them? The

Barbarians and Dastardlies that legend said lurked beyond the Wall? Were they the ones making those awful noises? Well, just in case, Rose backed away. No one knew much about them except Mr. Hump-Dumpty, who had described them as dreadful, gruesome, disgusting, and mean. She did not want to meet such creatures, thank you very much.

Still, she did want to find out more about those ant streams. But before she could try to get close enough to examine them more closely, she suddenly noticed a tall rectangular shape on the hedge behind her. It was the shape of the cabinet door that had transported her here. As she watched, the rectangle began to waver slightly, as if threatening to disappear. If it did, she'd be stuck here.

"No, wait!" Rose got a running start and leaped through the rectangle. And just like that, she was whisked back to the Cupboard.

Once she was inside Mother Hubbard's shop again, her knees began to wobble in reaction to what she'd just seen. She sank to the floor, feeling like she'd just been through a wind tunnel. Or some kind of a magic tunnel? Anyway, she was safely back! And so was Mother Hubbard. She was asleep at her desk and there was a hatbox on the floor by her feet labeled THE CANINE HATTERY.

Rose looked over at the cabinet she'd just traveled through. The door had shut behind her, and was already resizing itself into a small square. No way she'd ever fit back through it now. How disappointing!

Just then, she heard the grandfather clock over in the Great Hall bong twelve *bongs*. Lunchtime? Already? She slipped out of the Cupboard and made her way down the hall. Cupboard time must warp sort of like Library time did, she figured. Because while she'd been at the Wall, somehow she'd missed the rest of Scrying and third-period Calligraphy, too.

When she passed the Scrying room, she peeked in, but Ms. Wicked was gone. Would she be angry that Rose had missed the end of class and come back empty-handed? And what would she think if Rose told her what had happened? Spotting her handbook still on her desk, she went in and got it, then slipped soundlessly out into the hall again.

8
Cry Pie

When Rose got to the Great Hall, she found herself standing in the lunch line behind Cinda and Rapunzel, who were still not being very friendly.

Several students ahead of them all, Pea leaned out of line to look back at her. "Hey! There's a twig in your hair. Are you copying my style?" she asked. Grinning, she patted her own viney green hair. Then she reached the serving area and spun around to order her lunch.

"Oh," Rose reached up and felt the twig Pea had been talking about. It must've gotten caught in her hair when she fell through that hedge. She was glad Pea was still being nice. At least she had one friend left. But what would happen when Pea heard whatever rumors were going around about her?

She was dying to tell Cinda and Rapunzel about what she'd seen at the Wall. But since the door that had led there no longer did, she wouldn't be able to back up her words with proof. And from the way they had been acting today, she had a feeling that just telling them what she'd seen wouldn't convince them she was being truthful.

The two Grimm girls continued to ignore Rose as they all inched forward in line. Finally she confronted them. "What's going on?" she blurted. "I feel like almost everyone here has turned against me suddenly, but I don't know why."

Cinda and Rapunzel traded glances. Then Cinda spoke, saying, "Well, truth is that all the students understand how evil characters are part of the fairy tales and have a right to be in Grimmlandia just as much as we do. But the E.V.I.L. Society has done a lot of harm, and so —" She stopped short as if unsure how to continue.

"And so even though we like you, we aren't sure we should continue to hang out with you," Rapunzel finished for her. Cinda nodded, gazing at Rose as if Rapunzel's little speech explained everything.

"What are you talking about?" Rose asked them in confusion. At the same time a lump of sadness filled her throat. These girls were basically saying they didn't want to be her friends anymore. Maybe no one at GA did! "Haven't you read my tale? I'm not evil in it," she insisted desperately.

Cinda and Rapunzel just stared at her. Then they began to describe her tale, telling a variation of it that sounded suspiciously similar to the one Ms. Queenharts had told in class. Only in their version Rose and her family came off even worse than they had in Ms. Queenharts' retelling!

". . . After twelve fairies gave you gifts at your christening, the thirteenth fairy arrived. The one your dad didn't invite," Rapunzel was saying.

"She was a sweet innocent fairy, but your dad refused her an invitation because your mom was jealous of her good nature and pretty wings," Cinda went on matter-of-factly.

"And when fairy number thirteen showed up anyway, and fluttered over to coo at baby Rose — that is, at you — you spit up on her," added Rapunzel. "On purpose."

"Yeah, and then —" Cinda started to add.

But Rose had had enough. "Huh? No! That's all wrong!" She felt herself flush with sadness and anger, too. She liked these girls, so their attitude really hurt. And it double-triple hurt that they would believe the truly dislikeable Ms. Queenharts over her.

Suddenly, she reached the front of the lunch line. A wrinkled old hand shot into her line of vision. Its fingers held out a small plate to her.

"Care for a bit of dessert with your lunch, dearie?" a scary voice inquired. "A slice of my Sweet Potato Cry Pie?

You'll start sobbing with joy the minute you take a bite. It's that yummy."

Rose wasn't sure she needed pie to help her cry right now. She halfway felt like doing that already. She looked up into the eyes of Mistress Hagscorch, the cafeteria lady. Her white-gray hair was as wild and scraggly as the moss that grew at the edge of Neverwood Forest. She looked exactly like a storybook witch. And sounded like one, too.

When Rose didn't reply, Hagscorch picked up two other plates instead, each with a different dessert. "No? Then perhaps some Poisonless Peanut-Butter Pretzels? Or Reeky Raisin Roll-Ups? Hmm? What's it going to be?" she asked, waving the choices under Rose's nose.

Despite their horrid names, the desserts did all smell delicious. Still, Rose shook her head, too upset to eat. "I'm sorry. I'm n-not hungry!" With that, she slipped out of line and took off, walking fast to the exit doors of the Great Hall.

Out in the hallway, she happened to pass the trunker Ms. Jabberwocky had assigned to her. Good, she could stow her handbook there. Forever. She didn't want it. She wouldn't be taking classes here any more because she was leaving Grimm Academy. Right now. Forever. No matter what. She wasn't sure where she'd go, but she was not sticking around where she wasn't wanted.

She poked the key dangling from the chain around her neck into the trunker's lock, and quickly sang her code:

"Row, row, row your boat,
Gently down the stream.
Merrily, merrily, merrily, merrily,
Life is but a dream."

Her fingertip caught on the edge of her handbook as she went to place it inside the trunker. "Ow!" She'd gotten a paper cut.

Instantly, those sparkly, colored mists began to magically swirl in the air again. The fairies had arrived! She looked around to see if anyone else in the hall noticed them, but, as usual, no one seemed to. They were invisible to all but her.

"What happened to your finger?" the yellow fairy asked her worriedly.

"Paper cut, that's all," Rose muttered.

"Does it sting?" asked the purple fairy. She and the other fairies hovered near as Rose recited her locking code.

"Hush, you two. We've got more important things to discuss," began the pink fairy. But the minute Rose's face appeared in the small heart shape above her trunker's keyhole, the pink fairy got distracted, saying, "Ooh! How cute!"

"Bug off, please," Rose interrupted under her breath. "I'm not in the mood for your scoldings or advice, thank you all very *not* much. So just fly back where you came from. Or go bother someone who needs your help."

"But won't you please listen?" the purple fairy insisted.

The pink fairy nodded. "It's really important."

As the fairies kept trying to talk to her, Rose pressed her fingers to her ears. "Lalalalalala," she murmured, doing her best to drown them out. Finally, she spun around and ran, not caring who saw her. Any students who did would probably just think she was in a hurry because she was late for something, anyway.

Unfortunately, the fairies and their misty puffs were not so easily put off. They followed her as she left her trunker. In an attempt to lose them, she sped up and dashed out of the Academy. They trailed her outside, beating their little wings double-time to keep up with her. She ran faster and faster across the lawn, trying to escape them. After rounding a corner, she leaped to hide behind a haystack. She crouched low, waiting till the fairies flew past.

They hadn't noticed she'd given them the slip. Good. After waiting for her breath to slow, Rose rocked forward on her knees and peeked out, watching all three fairies disappear into the distance. Then she rocked backward on her heels, preparing to stand.

"Ouch!" She'd lost her balance and fallen to one side, leaning up against the haystack. She must've leaned against a sharp piece of hay that had gotten stuck in her skirt and was poking her. She twisted her skirt around to check.

Sure enough, she spotted a sliver sticking out of the fabric. However, it wasn't hay. The sliver glinted in the sunlight. It was straight, very thin, about two inches long, and *silver*. It was a sewing needle! In spite of her sadness, a half sob, half giggle escaped her. Because she'd literally just found a needle in a haystack.

"Well, at least you made me smile once today," Rose told it. She looked around. "How did you get out here in the hay, anyway?" Of course, the needle didn't reply.

Since she didn't want anyone else to be so unlucky as to get stuck by it, she tucked the needle in her pocket to discard later. She peeked out from her hiding place again. Not seeing the fairies, she leaped to her feet. Then she stood there uncertainly. To her left was the Academy. To her right were the stables.

There wasn't much time left till Friday if she really did plan to have one last grand adventure, she realized. So right then and there, she decided that she and Starlight would ride for the Wall that very afternoon. She'd check out what was going on with those ant streams and hopefully discover whatever evil plot was causing changes to the fairy tales. Maybe she'd even discover how to save all of Grimmlandia!

Then everyone at the Academy would change their tune about her. She'd be a hero. Her parents might even decide she was brave enough to become a knight, in spite of the risks. Spirits lifting a little at this notion, she took off running for the stables. Because it was now or never!

After crossing the lawn, Rose topped a few gentle hills, and then found the stables not far from Pink Castle. They were built out of big brown stones and wood that had been painted white.

Once inside the stables, she zipped down the center aisle of the barn and checked each stall. She spotted a brown horse with spots. A black horse with a star. A roan. A piebald. There! A gleaming horn was poking out of one of the stalls. She dashed over to it but found to her disappointment that it was the horn of a pink unicorn, not Starlight.

Seeing the stable boy, she stopped. "The white unicorn that came here Monday night. Where is he?" she asked.

"He went back with the silver-and-black coach that same night, Princess," the boy informed her. "Returned with his owners to a palace somewhere in southeastern Grimmlandia, I heard."

Rose's shoulders slumped in disappointment. Her parents had taken her unicorn back to the palace without even telling her? If she wrote and asked them why, she knew they'd say they'd done it to protect her from being pricked by his horn. And they'd been in a big hurry as they left with no time to let her know their decision. But still. Losing Starlight — her only friend from home — hurt worse than a toothache right now.

"Okay, thanks," she told the stable boy, giving him a wobbly smile. In a daze, she left the stables and wandered out to the lawn. There, she stood and swung around in a circle, not knowing what to do. She would miss Starlight more than she could say. And without him, she had no way to get to the Wall. That cupboard door wasn't there anymore to transport her, and the Wall was too far away to reach by foot. She felt the chance for one last great adventure slipping away.

But then determination surged anew inside her. There were still three more days before her twelfth birthday. Somehow she'd figure out a way to end her daredevil career on a high note!

And suddenly, a new thought came to her. Yes! It was the perfect way to prove to Cinda and the others that they were wrong about her. She'd simply go to the Grimmstone Library, get the Grimm book with her tale, and show it to them.

She was in no mood for a riddle, but after she roamed the halls and finally found the only doorknob in the school without the GA logo, it turned into a beaky gooseknob that demanded she answer one. It was super easy this time, though, as if the knob wanted to help.

"Which candle burns longer — a pink candle, a blue candle, or a white candle?" it asked.

"None of them," Rose guessed. "Candles always burn *shorter.*"

Snick! Without another word, the gooseknob magically changed itself into a round brass knob. Which meant she'd guessed correctly. A huge rectangle drew itself on the wall around the knob. It formed a door that stood several feet taller than her and was decorated with low-relief carvings of nursery-rhyme characters.

The library door swung open. Once through it, Rose rushed to Section *G*. And there in front of a shelf, she found Pea! She was standing there, reading the *Sleeping Beauty* tale in the great Books of Grimm.

When Pea looked over at her, her eyes were filled with a new wariness. "I just read your tale and . . ."

A feeling of doom crept into Rose. "Let me see that

book," she said, hurrying over to take a look at her tale for herself. To her surprise, it actually *was* different now.

"It's just like Cinda and the others said," she murmured in horror. The words in her tale indicated that she and her family had been inexcusably rude and purposely mean to the thirteenth fairy. In fact, not only had baby Rose spit up on the thirteenth fairy at her first birthday party, she'd supposedly even reached up with her tiny hand and slapped the fairy so hard that she knocked her right out of the air!

Rose looked up at Pea, aghast.

"This is awful! It's like what happened with Rumpelst — I mean with *Principal R's* tale. Mine's been changed, too, don't you see? Rewritten!"

Pea's forehead furrowed. "What are you talking about?" Her expression clearly seemed to say that Rose was either crazy or trying to trick her somehow.

"Oh, I forgot you weren't there. But Cinda and the others can tell you. Someone changed the principal's fairy tale, and now mine, too. Do you really not remember how my tale used to read?" she asked Pea.

Pea shook her head, the pretty, long green vines of her hair rustling.

"Think about it," Rose said, desperately trying to persuade her. "I was just a baby. How could I . . . *why* would I be so mean to a grown-up fairy?"

She looked down at the third page of her altered tale. Right before her eyes, more words appeared, added by an unseen hand: *Then the bad baby Rose bit the fairy — hard enough to leave a scar — and laughed!*

"What? No way!" she said, startled. She looked up at Pea. "Did you just see what happened?"

"I did!" said Pea, her eyes rounding in shock. "New words wrote themselves into your tale. But . . . how can that be?"

Rose sighed in relief. Finally! Someone believed her. She liked Pea and the other Grimm girls who'd befriended her, and couldn't bear for them to go on thinking of her as evil. Even if she was still planning to leave here as soon as she could.

"Look! It's doing it again," said Pea.

Rose turned the book slightly so they could both watch her tale in the process of being rewritten: *Finally, the thirteenth fairy felt she had no choice. Horrible little Rose had to be puni* — The rewriting stopped abruptly, but it was too late. They'd both seen.

"Punished," said Rose. "That's what it was about to write."

"Look at the ending," Pea said suddenly. She jabbed her finger at a place farther down the page. "The curse the fairy put on you just changed, too."

"Oh, no! Now it says that when I fall into a hundred-year sleep, the whole *Academy* will fall asleep, too!" said Rose.

Both girls gasped.

"How is this happening?" asked Pea.

"Quick, do you have a pen?" Rose asked. When Pea handed one over, Rose tried using it to correct her tale in the book. But the book wouldn't allow her to write in it. "If E.V.I.L. can change the tales, why can't we change them back?" she wondered in frustration.

The girls just stood there looking at each other, neither having any clue. "We'd better get to class," said Pea at last. Then she yawned. Poor thing never seemed to get enough sleep at night in that uncomfortable bed of hers.

Just then, Rose's stomach growled, which reminded her she hadn't eaten lunch. On the way out of the library, they found some snacks in the nearby *F* section on a shelf labeled FEAST. There was French bread, fudge, and many other *F* foods. Munching some fruit, Rose and Pea headed out of the library only to discover that the halls were empty of students.

"We must be late for fourth period," said Rose, figuring everyone else must already be in class. "I've kind of been dreading our Comportment class after what happened yesterday." Reluctantly, she started for the stairs that would take them down to the second floor.

"Wait. Maybe we don't have to go," said Pea. She stopped a boy who had just appeared, having entered the hall from the twisty staircase. "We've been in the library," Pea told him, when he drew close enough to hear. "What period is it now?"

"Sixth," he said easily, continuing down the hall without missing a beat.

Pea grinned at her. "Know what that means?"

Rose nodded, brightening. "Time sped up. It's sixth period!"

"Right! We missed Comportment. And fifth period, too! Don't worry, though. Missing classes because of library time is always an excused absence."

"Grimmtastic!" Rose was disappointed to have missed fifth-period Sieges class, but on the bright side, she'd also missed Comportment.

Pea laughed at how pleased she sounded, which made her feel happy. Things seemed back to normal between them. Now that she believed Rose hadn't turned evil.

As they headed down the hall, Rose remembered something. Her tower task was today! Looking over at Pea, she asked, "Um, do you happen to know where I can find the three Rub-A-Dub-Dub guys from the nursery rhyme? Ms. Jabberwocky said I'm supposed to help them sixth period on Wednesdays."

9

Candlesticks

Following the instructions Pea gave her, Rose made her way to Gray Castle, then wound downstairs till she found herself in a dungeon. She went along a hall until she saw what looked like the side of a small actual ship sticking out of the wall. Had it been wrecked on the shores of Once Upon River and simply been built into the castle's dungeon at some point? Looked like it. A small door had been cut into the ship's hull, and a round lifesaver-ring hung up on it. There were two words painted in red on the ring: *The Tub.*

Rose knocked once, then went through the door. Inside, she immediately saw three men no taller than she, all busily working in a neat, shipshape room.

"I'm looking for the candlemaker?" she announced, drawing their attention.

"I'm the butcher," said the first man, who was sharpening knives. "I'm the baker," said the second man, who wore a tall white chef's hat. She wondered if he supplied bread and stuff like that to Mistress Hagscorch's kitchen in the Great Hall. But then again, maybe she baked her own?

She went up to the third man, who was working over a big black pot of boiling water hanging above the flames burning in the fireplace. "Hi. You must be the candlestick-maker," she said. "I'm Rose. My tower task is to help you on Wednesdays, sixth period."

The candlestick-maker looked over at her and frowned. "That's odd. I didn't hear anything from the office about getting a helper. What are you supposed to do?"

"Help you make candles?" she guessed. "But I have to be honest. I'm not really all that interested in candlemaking."

His eyes rounded and he gasped, as if he couldn't believe anyone wouldn't kill to have such a fabulous job. He stared hard at her. "Well, this is a curious ball of wax. Why would you be assigned as my helper then?"

"The tower tasks often seem ill-suited at first, but almost always turn out to fit students they're assigned to," the butcher reminded him, still sharpening his knives. "She looks sharp as a tack," he added, nodding toward Rose. "I'm sure she's cut out for the job."

"I'm sure you'll catch on easy as pie," the baker encouraged her.

"Right. That's what —" Rose started to mention that the other Grimm Girls had said pretty much the same thing about tasks turning out to be a good fit, but then her throat tightened. She didn't want to think about them and how their feelings about her had changed.

To keep herself occupied, she watched the candlestick-maker tie six strings to a paddle and dip them into the steaming pot. After about a minute, he pulled the paddle up. The strings were now each covered with a coating of wax. So that's what was boiling in that pot, she realized. Not water. Wax.

"These strings are candlewicks," the candlestick-maker explained to her proudly. He was obviously totally into candlemaking. "You pull them out and allow the wax to cool between dippings." He lifted the paddle high, so she could see the newly wax-coated wicks dangling from it. "Dipping them into wax is a little tricky because the wicks float until they eventually get weighed down by more and more coats of wax. Don't worry. You'll get the hang of it. Just make sure . . ."

Eager to try her hand at this new skill, Rose nodded and reached for the paddle. Before he finished speaking, she dipped the wicks in the boiling wax again. Unfortunately, when she drew them back up, they had a mind of their own. The newly-coated wicks bumped into one another, instantly sticking together. Instead of six waxy wicks, the paddle now held a tangled ball of waxy string!

"Oh, no! I'm sorry. What did I do wrong?" she said, handing the paddle over to the candlestick-maker.

"I was going to instruct you not to let the wet candles touch each other, but you . . ." He looked exasperated. "Look, what did your tower task slip say exactly?"

Rose cocked her head, thinking, then told him, "It started out with the word *candles* but the rest of it was cut off by some crazy scissors in the Grimmstone Library," she admitted.

"Well, it's plain as steak on toast," said the butcher, overhearing.

"Clear as egg white on a soufflé," agreed the baker.

"Indeed," said the candlestick-maker, nodding. "I think you've come to the wrong place. You want the coach. Out on Gray Castle lawn."

"You mean the one who teaches Sieges class?"

All three men nodded. "His name is Jack," said the butcher. "Full name Coach Candlestick."

"As in the nursery rhyme, 'Jack Jumped Over the Candlestick,'" said the baker.

"A jumpy fellow, that one. Hops around like his feet are on fire at the slightest sound," added the candlestick-maker.

A light as bright as a candle went on in Rose's brain. "Oh! I get it," she said at last. "Thank you!" With a wave of farewell, she dashed off, making her way upstairs and outside Gray Castle. Her tower task was to help the coach with knight stuff? Well, that was more like it!

In minutes, she was out on the lawn. The coach was standing in front of a row of full-size, person-shaped dummies stuffed with hay, and he was lecturing a small group of armored students on knightly skills.

"Never assume you will hit your target. Because if you miss, you might wind up swinging your sword around and striking your own backside," he was saying.

Awesome! Just the kind of thing she hoped to learn about. Rose stood at the edge of the group, waiting till he'd finished his talk. When the students went off to practice, she ran up to him, but he was polishing his sword and didn't see her.

"I'm sorry I'm late!" she announced.

At the sound of her voice, Coach Candlestick leaped high in the air, eyes as big as Mr. Hump-Dumpty's egg-size ones. His nursery rhyme said he jumped over candlesticks, and based on how high he'd just leaped, he must be pretty good at it, she decided.

"Never creep up on me like that! Especially when I'm holding a sword," he scolded. Then he eyed her. "Aren't you in my fifth-period class?"

Rose nodded. "Yes, sorry. I missed it today because of time speeding up while I was in the library. Then I made a mistake and went to the candlestick-maker. But I'm here now because I'm your helper. I mean you're my tower task. I mean —"

Coach Candlestick's eyebrows slammed together. "Sixth period is Advanced Knight Training. And there is no room for *mistakes* in this class. One teeny error and . . ." He lunged forward, jabbing his sword blade into the nearest hay-stuffed dummy.

"Got it. Honestly, I'm so sorry!" Rose hoped he wasn't going to kick her out of her tower task before she even got started. She rushed to convince him. "I want to be a knight someday. So I promise, I'll be a very dedicated helper. I'm quite agile and brave and have an excellent sense of balance. I slide down banisters and never fall. I can ride my unicorn, no-hands. I even leaped around the tops of the shelves in the library my first day at GA."

Unfortunately, the coach looked unimpressed. "There's a difference between being a daredevil and being a knight," he told her bluntly. "However, I'll give you a chance, since you were assigned to me. So listen, watch, and do your task. And maybe someday, if you learn to focus that energy and determination of yours, you'll be admitted to Advanced Knight Training yourself."

With that, he began giving her instructions on the care of the armor and weapons. It seemed her task was going to involve a lot of polishing. That was okay with her. Because he'd said she could watch and listen to the training the whole time.

"Now we will practice sheathing and unsheathing our swords," the coach told the students a few minutes later. Rose kept her eyes peeled and her ears open. "The number one thing to remember is: Swords are sharp. When you pull one out, you could easily slice your arm. When you go to sheathe it, you could poke yourself by accident. There is no room for error, knights!"

The time spent at her tower task slipped by in what seemed like only one second. At the end of class, the knights-in-training all gathered in a circle and swore an oath, which she guessed they did at the end of each class.

"We promise to be loyal and brave," they chanted. "And to protect Grimm Academy and all of Grimmlandia against evil."

"I do," she murmured solemnly to herself as their words died away. Even though she wasn't part of the circle and wasn't a knight-in-training . . . yet, Rose memorized the words they'd spoken and played them over and over in her mind.

Coach Candlestick was right. She had already learned a ton of stuff just watching, listening, and helping. In the days to come, she might learn sword fighting, using lances in tournaments, and other knightly stuff. Things were looking up. Suddenly, she wasn't so anxious to leave the Academy. But how could she fix things so she could stay? She had to try. Because she'd just vowed to protect it!

At dinner in the Great Hall that evening, Pea helped Rose explain to Cinda, Red, Snow, and Rapunzel about her *Sleeping Beauty* tale being rewritten. And then Rose filled them all in on the trip she'd taken to the Wall via the Cupboard.

The girls hung on her every word, and once she'd finished, Red set down her fork with a clank. "I wonder if Ms. Wicked was trying to get rid of you? Maybe she knew where the mirror polish was in The Cupboard. Maybe she hoped you'd go through that door so the Dastardlies could somehow get you to go over the Wall from where you could never return."

Rose blinked, feeling a shiver sweep her. "Think she'd really do that?" And here she'd been worried she'd failed Ms. Wicked by not bringing back any polish!

Snow groaned, rolling her eyes. "You don't know my stepmom very well yet. But believe me, she is grimmbar-rassingly mega-evil."

The six of them all looked at one another, eyes wide with worry. Pea reluctantly said her farewells and headed off just then, saying that she'd offered to help a girl named

Mary Mary Quite Contrary with the pea patch in the Academy garden before it got dark. Rose promised to fill her in on the rest of their discussion later in their room.

As the bluebirds flew down to pick up their trays, Rapunzel said, "This situation is getting out of control. We've got to do something. Fast."

"But what?" asked Cinda.

"I think we need help," Rose told the girls as they all stood to go. "Who do you guys trust most around here? Grown-up-wise, I mean."

"Not my stepmom, that's for sure," Snow put in, grabbing her sparkly blue school bag from the bench beside her before they left the table and exited the Great Hall.

"Or Malorette and Odette," added Cinda. "My stepsisters," she added for Rose's information. "They go here, and we know for sure they're members of E.V.I.L."

"Thing is, it's hard to know just who we can trust," said Red.

"We could tell Principal R at least," said Rose. "He's not in the E.V.I.L. Society, is he?"

Rapunzel shook her head, her long, loose braids swaying with the motion. "Well, we're pretty sure he's not."

"I say we go talk to him," Snow said.

Classes were over, so the first-floor hall was empty of students when they stopped by the trunkers so Rose could get her handbook before they headed upstairs to the Principal's office on the fourth floor. She wanted to use it to study up on knight rules when she got back to her dorm that night. She was just about to say her trunker code when they heard voices drifting out from one of the classrooms.

"Yes, Ludwig. We're on it," said one of the voices. It sounded familiar, but Rose couldn't quite pinpoint who it belonged to. Still, she froze upon hearing the name of the banished Grimm brother, Ludwig. He was the head of the E.V.I.L. Society!

"I've got the students in my classes searching for loopholes," added another voice.

The girls glanced at one another, eyes rounding in surprise.

"That's —" Cinda started to whisper. But when Rapunzel put a finger to her lips, Cinda fell silent. They'd all recognized the second voice as Ms. Wicked's. Both speakers were apparently talking to E.V.I.L.'s leader.

But how could that be if Ludwig Grimm was still on the other side of the Wall? Rose pointed across the hall and a ways down to a door that stood half open, indicating that she thought the voices were coming from Ms. Wicked's room. The others nodded.

Snow slipped something from her school bag and set it on her head. Her magic tiara. *Be right back,* she mouthed silently to them, handing her bag to Cinda. Without waiting for a reply, she pressed the center jewel on her tiara and immediately went invisible.

Rose's jaw dropped at this amazing feat of magic. Then the voices began again. Quickly, she, Red, and Cinda hurried over and flattened themselves against the wall just outside Ms. Wicked's classroom door so they could listen in. Rapunzel went to the end of the hall to keep an eye out on the stairs and ensure that no one would unexpectedly catch them all spying.

When they were in position, they heard Ms. Wicked say, "— and once her curse goes into effect on Friday, Grimmlandia will be ours to do with as we like."

"With the whole Academy asleep, there'll be no interference for the next hundred years!" the other voice exulted. It was Ms. Queenharts, Rose suddenly figured out.

"At last, we'll break down the boundaries between our two worlds!" Ludwig's voice cackled. "E.V.I.L. will take over."

They were talking about *her* curse, Rose realized with a start. They planned to use its fulfillment as a way to take over Grimmlandia and somehow merge it with the Nothingterror beyond the Wall. But something about their plan didn't seem quite right to her. She was trying to put her finger on just what was wrong with it when Snow returned.

The girls moved to huddle a short distance away so their whispers wouldn't be overheard. "They're talking to the big mirror on Ms. Wicked's wall. And gazing into her crystal ball, too. But Ludwig just signed off to go break up a fight between a couple of Dastardlies," Snow reported after she went visible again.

"Mirrors are how they're able to communicate with him and send him stuff while he's banished to the Nothingterror," Cinda explained in a low voice to Rose.

"Yeah, remember how we told you E.V.I.L. stole some artifacts from the library a while back?" Red added quietly. "When the artifacts returned, they poured in through a magic mirror."

"Hide behind the door for a minute, you guys," said Snow. "I'm going to create a diversion over in Mr. Hump-Dumpty's room. If the two of them take the bait and go over there, zip into my stepmom's classroom and see what's up in that mirror and crystal ball if you can. I'll keep them busy for as long as possible. But when you hear two crashes in a row in Mr. Hump-Dumpty's room, run! It'll be my signal that they're coming back."

With that, Snow touched the jewel in her tiara and went

invisible again. A minute later, they heard a loud thump coming from Mr. Hump-Dumpty's classroom.

"Did you hear that?" Ms. Queenharts hissed from somewhere inside Ms. Wicked's room. "I think it came from Mr. Hump-Dumpty's room. But he's gone. I saw him leave earlier."

"Hmm. Let's go check it out," said Ms. Wicked.

Rose, Red, and Cinda hid behind the door as the two teachers hurried over to Mr. Hump-Dumpty's room. Then the three girls slipped inside the Scrying classroom to stare at the big mirror at the front wall. Wisps of air were forming all around them, long streams of ants passing out through the mirror to somewhere. Only they weren't ants at all. They were little black letters, forming words and phrases. Cinda gasped and then clapped a hand over her mouth. Everyone's eyes were wide as they gazed at the strange sight.

"These streams look just like the ones I saw going over the Wall," Rose whispered to the others. The streaming words said things like, "the king and queen's daughter" and "christening" and "fairy gave her beauty." She wrinkled her nose, thinking hard. "Why do these words sound so familiar? Oh! They're from my fairy tale! The way it was originally written, I mean."

She reached out and tried to capture some of the

streaming words. To stop them from leaving the realm through the mirror. But her hands passed right through them. It was like trying to grab air. Impossible!

Giving up on that, she hurried over to gaze into the crystal ball on Ms. Wicked's desk. It still displayed her *Sleeping Beauty* fairy tale.

Meanwhile, as the word streams left the room through the mirror, other streams of words passed them, coming in. The phrases coming *in* were unfamiliar. And badly written. Things like, "the baby poked the fairy in her bodaciously beautiful fairy eye" and "poor adorable sweetest-fairy-ever thirteen."

"Think this is how E.V.I.L. is changing your tale?" Red whispered. "By stealing Jacob and Wilhelm Grimm's words and replacing them with Ludwig's?"

Rose nodded. "I bet those horrible sounds I heard at the Wall were Dastardlies munching Jacob and Wilhelm's words as soon as they crossed into the Nothingterror. It must be what the Dastardlies do. Destroy words. Maybe even imagination, too."

"If they keep that up, more fairy tales and nursery rhymes will soon be changed or lost forever," said Cinda.

Crash! Crash! When Snow's two-crash signal came from the other room, the girls didn't wait to hear the *click, click* of high heels coming toward them.

Quickly, Rose grabbed another crystal ball from the shelf and switched it out with Ms. Wicked's, hoping to fool her. Then she handed Ms. Wicked's ball to Red, who put it in her basket as they all scurried back down the hall to join Rapunzel at the stairs. Snow joined them, too, and they raced up to the fourth floor, filling Rapunzel in on all that they'd seen and heard.

"We knew Ms. Wicked was in the E.V.I.L. Society," panted Cinda from beside Rose as the five girls finally entered the fourth-floor hall and made their way to the school office.

"Yeah, but now we know for sure that Ms. Queenharts is, too," said Snow as they reached their destination.

"So you see what we meant about not knowing who we can trust around here," Red told Rose. She reached out and rattled the office doorknob, then her face filled with dismay. "It's locked!"

Rapunzel let out a disappointed huff. "I guess we should have known Ms. Jabberwocky and Principal R would be gone. It's after dinner. We'll have to try and corner him after morning announcements tomorrow."

"So what should we do till then?" asked Red. "Time's running out." She glanced at Rose. "Not just for you, but for the whole Academy."

Rose leaned against t̲̲̲̲̲̲ ̲̲̲̲̲̲̲̲
head. "I know, and I'm so sorr̲ ̲

"It's not your fault. This is ̲̲
her earnestly, and the others gathe̲
ding reassuringly.

"Still, I can't help feeling responsible, ̲
Rose admitted. "I've put everyone here in d̲̲̲ ̲̲̲̲̲̲ ̲̲̲ud-
denly, she stopped speaking and straightene̲ ̲Because
she'd just remembered thinking that E.V.I.L. had gotten it
all wrong.

"Hey! I just realized there's a huge flaw in the E.V.I.L.
Society's plan!" she announced. "If the whole Academy falls
asleep for a hundred years like my altered tale says, so will
Ms. Wicked and Ms. Queenharts. And any other E.V.I.L.
Society members, too."

Rapunzel gasped and looked at the others. "She's right!"

"Yeah, good point," said Red. "The Society must have
figured out how to avoid that, though."

"Think they're planning to go hide somewhere else
before the Big Sleep begins?" wondered Cinda.

"Maybe. You guys could do that, too," Rose urged as the
girls began moving down the hall. "The whole school could.
Or maybe I should go back home to the palace . . . except I
don't know if that would change things since my tale has

the Academy will fall asleep instead

. Oh, this is all getting so confusing!"

Let's take a closer look at Ms. Wicked's crystal ball and see if that helps us figure anything out," suggested Snow. Quickly, Red pulled the ball from her basket and the girls gathered around to study it.

Rose groaned. "They've made more changes to my fairy tale. Now it says I actually stomped on the thirteenth fairy and called her rude names."

Rapunzel rolled her eyes. "That's dumb. You were a baby. You couldn't even speak!"

"Hey! What's that tiny asterisk?" asked Cinda, pointing.

Rose looked more closely. "Hmm. That wasn't there before. It's at the end of the phrase E.V.I.L. changed to say the whole Academy will fall asleep if the curse takes effect."

As the other girls squinted at the words in the crystal ball, Rose ran her fingertip down to the bottom of the page, locating the corresponding asterisk there, almost hidden in a decorative border around the text. Printed in tiny letters following the asterisk were these words, which she read aloud: "except for members of the E.V.I.L. Society."

Her shoulders slumped. "Know what this means?" she said looking up from the ball. "It means that E.V.I.L.'s rotten plan has no flaw after all. They excluded themselves from my curse. They're safe."

10

Wicked

With heavy hearts and nervous anticipation, Rose and Pea met Red, Cinda, Rapunzel, and Snow for breakfast in the Great Hall the next morning. Their plan was to talk to Principal R after announcements. However, when the musicians blew their golden trumpets and the students all stood to face the balcony, he didn't appear.

Long minutes passed, then the School Board helmet-heads chorused: "Hear ye, hear ye! Important announcement! Principal R has disappeared. Therefore, he has been relieved of his duties as head of the Academy effective immediately. For the time being, Ms. Wicked will be acting as principal in his place."

Murmurs filled the Hall, quickly rising to an uproar. No one could believe the news!

"The Rumpster's gone?" Rose heard Wolfgang mutter incredulously from where he sat beside Red.

"No more Grumpystiltskin?" Cinda said to the others.

"What could've happened to him?" Rapunzel wondered aloud.

Snow wrinkled her nose. "My stepmother is now Principal Wicked?"

The trumpets sounded again. *Ta-ta-ta-ta-ta-ta-tum!*

Along with everyone else, Rose looked back toward the second-floor balcony that overlooked the far end of the two-story Great Hall.

Click! Click! Click! Wearing her trademark high heels, Ms. Wicked appeared on the balcony. Stepping up to the railing, she spread her arms wide and called for quiet.

"Students of Grimm Academy! As you are no doubt thrilled to have learned, I will henceforth govern the school. Which means I'm allowed to change a few rules. So until further notice, no one will be allowed off the school grounds." She smiled a wickedly beautiful smile that sent chills down Rose's back. "For safety reasons only, of course," she added with fake-sounding sweetness.

Rose gasped, then in a whisper loud enough so the other five girls would hear, she said, "That's to make sure everyone will be here to fall asleep if the curse takes effect."

"This means no venturing into Neverwood Forest," Ms. Wicked went on. "No going home to visit your families."

"What about trips to Maze Island or Heart Island?" called out Snow's crush, Prince Prince.

146

"Those are officially part of the Academy, and will be allowed," said their new principal. "However, outbursts such as yours are *not* allowed while I'm in charge here. Two demerits!"

"Oh, no!" murmured Snow. Leaning out of line to glance back at Prince Prince a dozen seats back, she sent him a sympathetic glance.

As students left the Great Hall for their first-period classes, rumors flew among them about where the principal could have disappeared to and why he'd been immediately removed from his duties. After first stopping off at her trunker, Rose reached Threads class to find that Red and Cinda were already there.

"On the way to class, I heard a rumor that Principal R had one too many temper tantrums, so the School Board ordered him to take some time off for an Anger Management class," Red told them.

"And I heard someone say he had a fit over the spinning-the-straw problem and whirled around till he broke his leg," said Cinda. "So he went to see a special doctor in another part of the realm until it heals."

"I heard that he got locked up in the Pink Castle dungeon for some crime," Rose put in. "Maybe for selling off school valuables because the magic straw hasn't worked out."

"I don't know for sure about the leg part or the anger class," said Cinda. "But I think Rapunzel would've mentioned seeing him in the dungeon if that were true. Her bedroom's down there, so I think she'd notice."

"All I know is, I don't like the new rules," said Red.

"Oh! My needle snapped," said Cinda just then. By now, the girls had finished their crochet projects and moved on to stitchery. Ms. Muffet and Ms. Spider were teaching them to do a decorative scallop stitch.

Cinda stood to go fetch another needle, but Rose stopped her. "Wait! I've got one." She pulled the needle she'd found in the haystack from her pocket. She'd placed it in a small box, which she now handed to Red who handed it to Cinda. "Found it yesterday, and I was going to stow it with the sewing supplies here in class today. With all the excitement, I almost forgot."

Cinda took the needle, saying thanks. But after a moment, she huffed and said, "It won't let me thread it."

"Let me try," Red took it from her. Eventually, she gave up, too. "Must be enchanted or something. I can't thread it, either."

"Weird," said Rose. She took the needle from Red, and then poked one end of the thread toward the opening in the needle. It slipped right through.

She looked at the others. "Beginner's luck?" Suddenly the needle jumped from her fingers and hovered over her lap, like a buzzing bee.

The girls stared at it. "Think maybe it wants to stitch something?" asked Cinda.

"Here." Red tossed the cloth she'd been using to practice the scallop-stitch over onto Rose's lap. Instantly, the needle began stitching words upon it all on its own. GUESS MY NAME.

Rose drew in a surprised breath, staring at the needle. "You have a name?"

"Know what I think? I think that needle is your charm," Cinda told her. "You know, like Snow's tiara. The one that made her invisible yesterday?"

"I agree," Red told Rose, nodding. "Because charms only work for the person they're meant for. Like my basket. It won't fetch anything for anyone but me."

Cinda lifted her hem slightly to show she was wearing her glass slippers. "Yeah, and these only fit me and lead *me* places. No one else."

"Having my own magic charm would be grimmawesome," said Rose. "But I'm not sure a needle is quite right for me. Even one with a name." She heard the doubt and disappointment in her own voice. The other girls' charms seemed much more fun and seemed to fit their personalities more than a needle fit hers.

"She's right, come to think of it," said Red. "I mean, a needle is about the sharpest thing there is besides maybe a dagger or scissors. And her curse will put her in danger of sharp things. Doesn't make any sense."

"Also, I'm not really that good at sewing," Rose put in. "And I'm not that interested in getting good at it, to tell you the truth."

"Yeah, Rapunzel's not either," Red sympathized. "I can imagine how she'd feel if she'd gotten a needle as her magic charm. Still, don't worry. I'm sure it can do wondrous magic."

"And you'll figure out all it can do as you go along," said Cinda.

"But first, it seems I'll have to figure out its name," said Rose. She stared at the needle, taking a guess. "Tweedle Needle?" The needle sewed the words: GUESS AGAIN. Rose looked at the other two girls, who offered guesses, too.

"Stitchy?" suggested Cinda.

"Pointdexter?" asked Red.

For the remainder of class, as they worked, the three of them tried about a hundred more name guesses such as Needlenose and Silver. After a while it got silly and they were trying names such as Sew-Sew and Stick-em-up. But each time, the needle simply pointed to the words it had sewn: GUESS AGAIN. They'd come up with nothing by the time class ended, so Rose boxed up the needle and headed to her next class — Scrying.

There, more rumors flew about the principal's where-abouts until Ms. Wicked arrived to begin class. She didn't address the rumors, but instead spoke to the students in a snooty tone, saying, "As you are all aware, I have been cho-sen from among all the teachers here to become principal of Grimm Academy. It's quite an honor." She caught sight of her reflection in her large wall mirror just then and paused to tuck a curl in place.

Wait a minute, thought Rose. There was something dif-ferent about that mirror today. It wasn't as tall or as wide and its frame was all wrong. It wasn't the same mirror that usually hung there! Had Ms. Wicked guessed that someone had been snooping in her classroom yesterday? Maybe. After all, they had taken her crystal ball, and the substitute probably hadn't fooled her. To avoid anyone else tampering with her magic stuff, she must've moved that mirror some-where safer.

Turning from the mirror, Ms. Wicked went on. "You shall continue to look for loopholes using the crystal balls. However, due to the new time demands of my additional principal duties, I'll need to assign a helper in each of my classes to do some of my teaching work." Her gaze roved the class. When it lit upon Rose, Ms. Wicked lifted an arm and pointed a finger right at her. "You, there. You'll be my helper."

Rose sat up straighter, surprised. "Wh-what do you want me to do exactly?"

"I didn't have time to put the crystal balls out for everyone before class, so please go pick some out and distribute them to all the students. And be quick about it." The teacher flicked her fingers toward the shelves, indicating that she should scurry over there and get started.

Rose stood and went to the shelves to load a bunch of crystal balls on a tray. Her mind raced, trying to think of a way to thwart Ms. Wicked's plans. Because the more students continued to work on this loophole-finding project of hers, the quicker the fairy tales and nursery rhymes were going to be destroyed. And eventually that meant the Wall would fall and Beasts and Dastardlies would pour into Grimmlandia from the Nothingterror. She shivered at the thought.

Noting that the crystal balls were all lined up on a single shelf, Rose got an idea. Did she dare? Yes! When the teacher wasn't looking, she purposely picked up one end of the shelf and knocked it askew. "Oops!" she said.

Crash! Dozens of magic crystal balls went bouncing and bumping across the floor, rolling under chairs and knocking against walls. Students shrieked and giggled in surprise. Some dodged the balls, while others tried to recapture them and round them up.

Ms. Wicked leaped from her chair, annoyed, to say the least. "What have you done? I had planned to enlist the help of all of my classes in my current project. But now . . ." She bent and randomly picked up one ball in each hand to study them closely. Noticing the new chips and cracks in them, she gritted her teeth. It was damage Rose had done.

"I'm so sorry!" Rose said, making a good pretense of innocence as she apologized profusely.

"Well, I suppose now we must all spend the day repairing the balls instead of completing the assignment I had planned," Ms. Wicked said sourly. Her narrowed gaze roved the class. "Get to it!"

Then she turned back to Rose. "Your days are numbered, anyway," she muttered snarkily in a voice low enough that the rest of the class wouldn't hear.

"What?" asked Rose, not sure she'd heard right.

The teacher only smiled a beautifully wicked smile, which made Rose think she knew something Rose didn't. Still, as the class set to work, she was pleased to know she'd managed to slow down the number of words escaping from any new tales by damaging the crystal balls. It seemed the best she could do for now. She did her repairs on the balls slowly and badly, hoping others would do the same. It was tedious work, and class dragged on for what seemed like hours. Finally, the clock bonged, setting them all free.

Rumors about the principal continued to swirl in her third-period class, and at lunch as well. But by fifth-period Sieges, Catapults, and Jousting class, no one seemed closer to knowing if there was truth to any of the rumors.

So Rose turned her mind to class, because today Coach Candlestick had promised some real action. They would begin learning fencing!

At the start of the period, each of them had grabbed a long, lightweight weapon called a foil, which was thinner than any sword and more flexible than a spear. Students were to hold it like a sword, and the object was to poke an opponent's torso (but not their arms or legs) with the tip end of the foil in order to make a score. Of course, their practice foils were made of stiff, but harmless, reeds, instead of real steel. Still, they all wore thickly padded shirts and protective face masks to avoid injury.

Fencing was an exercise in quick thinking and agility, she quickly discovered. Qualities that were important for any knight to possess, according to the coach. After practicing a few moves, they put them into action.

As her match with Knightly began, he got right to the *point*. "Do you know what's up with Principal R going missing?" he asked her. At the same time, he thrust his foil forward, going on the attack.

"No. Do you have a theory?" she replied, knocking his blade aside with hers in a move called a parry.

"My guess is he was dismissed because the School Board decided he couldn't be trusted for some reason," said Knightly.

"What? And Ms. Wicked can?" Rose scoffed. She executed a move called a riposte, going in for another try. The tip of her reed-blade touched his padded shirt and she scored a point.

"It's because of his fairy tale. It seems to have somehow changed . . . for the worse," Knightly said. "Good job, by the way," he added, complimenting her point.

"Thanks," Rose said absently. So not only had the word gotten out about the changes in her tale, people knew about the changes in the principal's, too. No doubt E.V.I.L. had made even more changes to the *Rumpelstiltskin* tale — changes to cook the principal's goose in the eyes of the School Board. She wondered what Knightly thought about *her* changed tale. He hadn't said anything, and wasn't acting any differently toward her. So she certainly wasn't going to bring it up.

They continued on, each scoring points against the other and proving to be well matched opponents, till class ended. As they took off their padding later, a little notebook fell from Knightly's pocket.

Rose picked it up with the point of her foil and flicked it over to him. He took it from her, staring down at it. After a minute he confided, "I wrote a story about Principal R's disappearance. A made-up one about what might've happened to him." He sounded almost embarrassed to admit all this. And, in truth, it was surprising.

"Really? I didn't know you like to write. I'd love to read it," she hinted. He shrugged and stuck the notebook in his pocket. They talked about other stuff then, all the way into Gray Castle. There, he seemed to reach a decision. Pulling out the notebook, he handed it to her. And as they moved toward their sixth-period classes, she read the first page.

Once she'd finished, she looked up at him. "This is really good!" she told him.

He smiled slightly. "Hey, don't sound so surprised."

"I'm not. I mean, I just didn't know you could write like . . . like the Grimms."

He shrugged, but Rose could tell how much what she'd said pleased him. This was important to him, she realized. And suddenly, she remembered that first morning here at GA when she'd seen him writing in his little book, a faraway expression on his face.

"Wait. This is your dream, isn't it?" she guessed. "To write. Not to become a knight."

Knightly shrugged again, but she sensed she was on the right track. They were getting close to her history class by now, so she paused by her trunker and opened it, hoping he'd keep talking.

"It's not really up to me," he went on, waiting beside her as she pretended to dig around in her trunker for something. "My brother Midknight will one day take my father's place and rule our castle in Grimmlandia. And Goodknight will go into politics. But as the third son, my family expects me to become a knight."

"Which is a respectable and honorable, not to mention exciting, profession," she hastened to put in. "But just not what you want, am I right?"

"Right. My parents want me to become a full-time knight, and I can't let them down. Best I can hope for is to be a part-time writey-knighty," he joked lamely, taking his notebook back and stowing it in his pocket as they moved on toward her class. "Still, it's cool to know that you think this is good. I haven't shown anyone else."

Rose kept thinking about Knightly and his dream all through sixth-period History. It was so unfair. Why couldn't he do what he loved? Write! And why couldn't she do what she loved? Become a knight! Sometimes parents were a trial. Life threw you curveballs, too. Or in her case, more like a curseball.

After classes that day, Red arrived late to dinner in the Great Hall. Flinging herself into her seat, she announced in typical dramatic fashion that she'd been called up to try spinning the principal's straw into gold.

"Ms. Queenharts is in charge of the project now that the Rumpster's gone. And honestly, Pea was right," Red complained. "That straw does not want to be spun. It jumped from my hand, and when I tried to grab it again it kept wiggling away like a fish in a stream. Impossible. So basically, I failed. It was a disaster."

Rose was barely listening, though. She was worried about too many things, especially her curse and the changing fairy tales. And, hey, where were those three fairies? She hadn't seen them since yesterday. She stuck her hand in her pocket and toyed with the box that held her needle.

Ever since Threads class, she'd tried experimenting with it. In Scrying, she'd realized it didn't need to be threaded in order to write messages. It could make its own magical thread somehow. In Calligraphy, she'd used it to sew-write messages on paper, but a pen could do that just as well. Not the greatest magic ever by a long shot. But it seemed to be all the magic the needle would perform until she guessed its name.

In Comportment, she thought maybe it had brought her good luck because Ms. Queenharts, who was busy helping out with the straw-spinning project now, had temporarily been replaced by a substitute teacher. Still, when Rose hadn't figured out its name and her needle didn't really do anything else by History class, she had pretty much decided her charm was a bust!

As she went to bed that night, she couldn't help feeling doomed. Her birthday was tomorrow. Her daredevil life would most definitely have to come to an end. She'd have to become a wimp. No more hopping around the tops of bookshelves or racing around on her unicorn. No more knight training.

How was she going to bear it? She'd have to, though. For the sake of all GA, her friends, and the survival of Grimmlandia!

11

Cursed

At precisely midnight, the Hickory Dickory clock bonged twelve bongs. With a gasp, Rose sat up in bed, awakened from a sound sleep.

Twelve bongs for twelve years. It was her birthday! The curse had officially gone into effect. She didn't feel any different, though. She lay down again. But unable to return to sleep, she was awake until nearly dawn, thinking hard.

Eventually, all that thinking paid off. She got an idea. A splendid one. One that might even save the Academy from certain doom! Or from a hundred-year sleep, anyway. Same thing, really. Because if the whole school went to sleep, E.V.I.L. would have way too much time to destroy the fairy tales. When the school eventually woke up, all would be changed. Undoubtedly for the worse.

Caw! Suddenly, a crow flew in the open window at the end of her dorm room. It dropped a message marble on Rose's pillow, then winged away again, out the window.

Leaping from the covers, she took the marble and scrambled down the ladder at the end of her bed. After lighting a candle, she read the words that flashed across the marble's surface, one after another. It was a summons to try to spin the straw into gold! Huh? So early? The sky outside was barely even pink yet. What could this mean?

Quickly, she got dressed, careful not to wake Pea. Before she left her dorm room, she stared at her needle where it lay glinting on her desk. She'd need it in order to put her splendid idea into action. She reached for it, then snatched her hand back, suddenly fearful. What if she pricked herself? What if — No! She would not let E.V.I.L. get to her like this. It was exactly what they wanted. Determination filled her and she carefully picked up the needle, put it in its box, and tucked it in her skirt pocket.

Taking the candle, she crept from her dorm. Going down the twisty stairs, she then ran up and down halls, looking for the gooseknob. For once, she kept an eye out for those mists actually hoping to run into the fairies. Maybe they had news of the principal or could help her with the needle's name. Naturally, now that she wanted them to come around and give her advice, they were nowhere to be found.

When she eventually found the library gooseknob, it asked a riddle as usual. "How are a tale and a tail similar?" it demanded.

"Each can be short or long?" Rose guessed right away. It was another easy one, like the candle riddle had been. *Super* easy this time, as if the knob really, really wanted her to hurry inside and put her splendid plan into action. And after she'd answered correctly, the library door drew itself on the wall more quickly than usual, too.

Once inside the library, she zipped down one aisle and then another making a beeline to Section *G*. The library was strangely smaller, so it didn't take long to get where she was going. The Grimm girls had told her it could change size and she wondered if it, too, was trying to help her execute her plan. Soon, she was pulling down the book that contained her *Sleeping Beauty* fairy tale from a shelf. Sitting on the floor, she set the book in her lap and opened it. Then she pulled the little box from her pocket and plucked her needle from it.

Would her plan work? She lifted the last page of her altered tale, and poked the point of her needle at it. The needle slipped through the vellum paper. So far, so good. Carefully, so as not to prick herself, she stitched a big *X* over a five-letter word on the page and stitched in seven new letters to take its place. As she stared at what she'd done, something fell on the book from high above.

Caw! She looked up to see another crow. Quickly, she read the message marble it had dropped. It was another summons to come spin the straw. Setting her book back on its shelf, she told her needle, "Fingers crossed that your stitching works. Right, um, Needle Ned?" When the needle didn't respond, she kept on randomly guessing more names. "Threadhead? Poker?" Still no luck.

Suddenly, she heard tiny voices calling her. "Help! Help!"

Were those her fairies? Filled with worry for them, Rose whirled around in a panic. "Where are you?" she called. She followed the voices to Section *S*. The same section where the magic straw was located, according to Pea and Red. The tiny voices led her into a door along one wall labeled STAIRS. She pushed through the door, to find twisty stone stairs that seemed to wind upward forever.

She started up, calling to the fairies. "I'm coming!" Finally, she reached the top. There, she entered a round tower room with a small window on one side. In the center of the room, stood a spindle. A single straw lay on it. There was no Ms. Queenharts. Still, it was obvious what she was supposed to do. Or try to do. Spin that straw into gold. Pea and Red had said it was impossible. And she should really stay away from that sharp spindle now that she was twelve. But where were the fairies?

Hearing them call again, she turned to see a big picture hanging on the far wall with a drape covering it. She went over and whipped the drape away. Then she drew in a sharp breath. It wasn't a picture at all. It was Ms. Wicked's wall mirror from Scrying class!

And within the mirror, she saw an image of the Wall. More words and letters began slowly streaming in and out of it, causing cracks to form. An eye appeared in one crack. A few fingers poked through. Something was trying to climb through the quickly forming cracks in the Wall and into Grimmlandia. Beasts? Dastardlies? Ludwig? All of the above? It was just as she and the Grimm girls had feared.

Feeling the needle twitch in her fingers, Rose realized she still held it. And it seemed to be trying to tell her something. "You think you can stitch glass?" she guessed. "Well, okay. Worth a try." She drew closer to the mirror and began whipstitching. To her surprise, it actually worked! It seemed her needle could stitch more than paper and fabric.

As she sewed the cracks shut, she could hear Beasts and Dastardlies grunting and groaning on the other side. She could smell their fishy, moldy-smelling breath coming through the cracks. "*Let us in*," they moaned.

"No way!" she muttered. In no time, her needle had stitched the cracks closed and she could no longer hear or smell them. Thank grimmness!

But now she noticed there was a long rope slung over the top of the Wall so it hung down along its front. It began to inch upward. A stoppered bottle appeared, tied on the rope's end. And the three fairies were trapped in the bottle. No, not just three. As many as a dozen!

"Help!" they cried in their tiny fairy voices. In minutes, they would be pulled into the Nothingterror!

"What should I do?" she called to them.

"Indeed, what *can* one such as you possibly do?" taunted a new voice. Rose turned to see yet another fairy hovering in the air between her and the door. This one was gray and grumpy-looking.

"Remember me?" the fairy asked, flitting closer.

Rose shook her head.

"Name's Thirteen. Fairy Thirteen. I'm the one your family didn't invite to your christening," said the gray fairy. "Big mistake." She came closer, flying in sharp back-and-forth zigzags until she hovered between Rose and the mirror. Meanwhile, over in the mirror, the bottle of fairies inched higher and higher along the Wall.

"I'm sorry," Rose told Thirteen. "My parents weren't trying to be impolite. Honest."

The fairy only arched an eyebrow. *Humph!* Then she gestured a tiny hand toward the spinning wheel. "Try your hand at spinning, won't you? If you succeed where others have failed, I'll forgive you and your family at long last.

And not only that! You could be the very one to save the Academy."

"Think so?" Rose asked innocently, as if she weren't fully aware of what this fairy was really up to. She looked over at the spindle. Its tip was sharp and gleamed dully in the dawn's early light. She had to think of something fast. To save those fairies and herself.

"Go on," urged the gray fairy, flitting around her in a tizzy now. "Touch it! Spin the straw into gold! Be a hero and save your little school friends. That's what a knight would do. And you want to be a knight, don't you?"

"How did you know?"

Just then the needle in Rose's hand twitched again. When she lifted it higher to gaze upon it, the fairy laughed. "Ha! You're going to fight me — and all of E.V.I.L. — with a tiny needle?"

"She's right," Rose whispered to the silver sliver in her fingers. "Thanks for trying to help, but you're just too . . . needle-teeny. I mean, you're too —" But before she could tell the needle that she'd actually meant to say it was too teeny to help much, the needle flashed brightly.

Zzzpht! It sprang longer, and longer. And longer still. Until it became a . . . sword! A real, amazing one. Though it had a flat sharp blade it was surprisingly lightweight and easy for Rose to hold. Almost like it had been made for her.

Sounding nervous for the first time now, the thirteenth fairy cried out a name. "Wandini!"

At this, the wand the fairy held grew as long as a sword, too. Hers must've also been lightweight, for the small fairy had no trouble wielding it. *Zzzpht! Zzzpht!*

A battle began. Rose and the fairy whacked and clanged, circling the room, each trying to win. *Clang! Clink! Clang! Clink!* It was sword against wand. It was good against evil!

The fairy gave a mighty swing of her magic wand, knocking Rose toward the spindle. For a little fairy no bigger than a melon, she packed a wallop.

Thinking fast, Rose spun around and swung her sword like a bat, whacking her opponent with the flat of her blade . . . and sending her flying out the tower's window. *Whoosh!*

The fairy's wand stayed behind. Instantly, it shrank to a small size and dropped to the floor. *Clink!*

Rose whirled to gaze at the mirror, fearing the worst. The fairy bottle teetered at the very top of the Wall now, dangling from the rope. Another tug and it would disappear over the Wall into the Nothingterror.

"No!" Rushing over, she swung her blade at the mirror, whacking it, too. *Crack!* It shattered into a zillion pieces. And, somehow, that released all twelve fairies trapped there. They came spilling out of the mirror in a rainbow of colors. The pink, yellow, and purple fairies were among them and flitted over to Rose, thanking her.

But she saw them as if through a dreamlike fog. "S-something's wrong," she murmured dizzily. She lifted her hand and looked at it. There was a drop of blood on her finger. *Oh no!* She'd pricked it on the spindle as she fought Fairy Thirteen!

"Ow!" she said. It would be her last word before the curse took effect. With it, she fell to the floor, asleep. And she wasn't the only one.

At the very same moment, everyone at the Academy, most of whom had just risen to begin their mornings, suddenly fell back asleep as the curse affected them, too. She saw them in her dreams.

Over in Pearl Tower, Snow, dressed in a blue nightgown, dropped to her knees on the blue polka-dotted rug in her dorm room and fell into slumber when the curse kicked in. Cinda, wearing a pink robe and carrying a pink towel, was on her way to the shower. The towel tumbled from her fingers as she sleepily slid to the floor, her cheek pillowed on one arm. And back in Emerald Tower, Pea had overslept, and simply turned over to continue dozing.

Rapunzel had gone to sit on the steps just outside her dungeon room to drink a cup of tea. Now her cup clinked to the stone step, cracking as she slumped against the stone wall next to her. As for Red, she had risen early and was baking something. It looked like a cake. And she had whipped up frosting in Rose's favorite color. Lavender. *Mmm.* She hoped the cake didn't burn, for Red was now seated at the counter in the center of Pearl Tower Dorm, her head on her folded arms, asleep.

Ms. Wicked had just risen and was staring at herself in a mirror (of course!). She was taking spiky black rollers out of her beautiful hair, and her face was covered with white, gooey face cream. Without her makeup and fancy clothes, she didn't look so beautiful now. However, unlike the others at Grimm Academy, she looked wide-awake. And she was smiling, as if she knew what was going on around her. Thinking that E.V.I.L. had won.

In a cozy room lined with bookshelves, Mr. Hump-Dumpty was snoozing away in a chair in what had to be his living quarters. And he was wearing pj's with little egg-shaped smiley faces on them. Which was totally out of character! Out in the stables, a boy had fallen asleep. So had all the horses. One by one, most everyone at the Academy fell asleep.

And less than two hours later . . . they all woke up again! All except Rose.

In her dreams, Rose could see them rising, one by one, each wondering what had just happened. Students and teachers were walking around a bit dazed because they'd just woken and didn't know where the time had gone.

Still, Rose slept on. But why? She didn't understand it. She'd changed things so this wouldn't happen to her, or so she'd thought. After all, everyone else at the Academy had awakened.

"Where's Rose?" Snow asked Pea at breakfast. But no one knew. As the hours passed, their worry grew. Her friends began searching for her.

Then Pea got an idea as she was talking with the other girls at dinner. "Mother Hubbard has a dog!" she blurted. They would get the dog to help track her down, they decided. Once they'd convinced Mother Hubbard, her dog led them to the library, to the fairy tale book. And at last, they arrived in the tower.

"Rose!" "There she is!" "It's her!" Pea, Rapunzel, Cinda, and a small crowd of other GA students gathered around her where she lay on the stone floor.

"Why didn't she awaken when the rest of us did?" Rose heard Cinda ask. But her voice seemed faraway and dream-like for Rose still saw this all in a dream.

Then something touched her face. It was Mother

Hubbard's dog, Prince. He'd licked her cheek. She stirred, her eyelashes fluttering. And just like that, she woke up. Pushing onto one elbow, she gazed around at all the faces in the room.

"She's awake!" Pea cried in delight.

"It was the dog that woke her, " said Rapunzel.

Rose sat up and the dog immediately jumped into her lap. She laughed as she hugged him to her. "Yeah. His name is Prince. I guess all that was needed to break my sleep was a kiss on the cheek from a totally adorable, corkscrew-tail prince of a dog," she said. Everyone laughed.

"Sleeping Beauty has been found and she's awake at last. Spread the word," someone toward the back of the room called out. Some students obediently peeled off from the crowd to race down the winding stairs.

"How long was I asleep?" Rose asked. Then she yawned, which made Pea yawn, which made everyone laugh again.

"All day," said Snow, who'd joined the group in the tower along with Red.

"The rest of us only slept about an hour and forty minutes," Red added. "No telling how long you'd have slept if not for that pooch."

When Mother Hubbard called her dog away, Rose glanced around the room for the fairies, but they were nowhere to be found. Had she only dreamed them? The thirteenth fairy's wand was missing, as was the cracked mirror.

But then Rose's gaze found her needle. It lay only a foot away on the stone floor and was still sword-size. So she hadn't dreamed *everything*!

"Needle-Teeny?" she said, speaking to it softly. She'd guessed that was its name, and she must've been right. For upon her words, it shrank to needle size again. *Zzzpht!*

As she tucked it inside its little box and stowed that in her pocket, she explained to her friends how she'd used it to stitch a change into the *Sleeping Beauty* tale. "Turns out this needle can stitch just about anything. Including glass and paper," she told them. "So in my fairy tale in the library, I *X*-ed out the word 'years' and stitched in the word 'minutes.' The curse of one hundred *years* became one hundred *minutes*. An hour and forty minutes, like Red said you all slept. Only, I still needed Prince's kiss to end the curse."

"Well, I'm glad you finally woke, because otherwise you would have totally missed your birthday!" Red exclaimed in a happy voice.

"Yeah! Now that your curse is broken, let's party!" said Pea. Cheers for this idea sounded from the crowd and they began to make their way out of the tower single file.

Rose had just started to push to her feet, when suddenly, a hand slipped into hers. A boy's hand, helping her up. It was Knightly. Not that she needed help. Still, it was nice of him. She smiled her thanks.

As they all left the turret room and started through the library, they passed Ms. Wicked. She looked startled for a moment, then shot Rose a fierce look. She was obviously annoyed, knowing she and E.V.I.L. had been bested, but not understanding how. Rose just grinned and sent her a happy little wave.

She and her new friends all gathered for the cake that Red had made outside in a fabulous garden that magically grew flowers in ready-made bouquets. "I saw this cake in my dream. It's beautiful!" raved Rose. Turned out that it hadn't been in the oven when Red fell asleep after all, but had only been sitting on a cooling rack before being frosted.

Pea, Cinda, Rapunzel, Red, and Snow wished Rose a happy birthday and lavished her with simple, sweet gifts of hair ribbons and decorations for her room that they'd made for her. As news spread of her awakening, more and more students came to wish her well. But not everyone did. Some still looked wary.

It was because most of her tale remained changed, as in wrong, Rose realized. And she didn't think there was enough stitching to ever make it completely right again.

She'd try, but no matter what she did, there might always be those who would believe her to be evil. So what, though?

In her heart, *she* knew the truth. And her real friends knew it, too. That she wasn't evil and never had been. With their support, she would stay strong and confident and persevere. Because that's what heroic knights did.

As the party wound down, Rose noticed colored lights hovering at the edge of the garden. Drifting away from the party, she wandered toward them, only to discover that they weren't lights at all. They were fairies! Twelve of them. They flitted around her, sparkling and winking as they thanked her for saving them from the mirror.

"We were at your christening," the fairies told her. Then they began to introduce themselves and tell her the gifts they'd given her when she was born. They floated gently around her head, darting quickly now and then so she had to turn her head this way and that to see which one was speaking.

After the first nine fairies had spoken in turn, the tenth fairy piped up. The pink one. "I'm Blush," it said. "I gave you the gift of beauty."

"I'm Violet," said the eleventh, purple fairy. "I gave you curiosity."

"I'm Sunny," said the chicken-yellow twelfth fairy. "I

meant to give you the gift of bravery. Then she smiled. "However, I think you found that gift yourself."

"Sunny gave you a more necessary gift at your christening, though, don't you agree?" Blush asked Rose. "She changed Pruney's curse."

"Pruney?" echoed Rose.

Darting closer, Violet interrupted. "Pruney is the thirteenth fairy's name, didn't you know? Her original curse was that you would prick your finger and *die*."

"Luckily, I hadn't yet given you a gift when she burst in uninvited," Sunny said, taking up the story. "I couldn't reverse her curse after she made it, but I was able to soften it. So that you'd sleep for one hundred years. I only wish I'd thought of using 'minutes' instead, like you did."

"No! It's okay. I mean, you saved me. All of you. Thank you, oh, thank you, for your gifts!" Rose told them. Hearing someone call her name from the garden, she started to wish the fairies good-bye.

"Wait! There's something we've been trying to tell you all this time, but you kept shutting us down," Blush rushed to say.

Sunny nodded. "Pruney is helping the E.V.I.L. Society."

"You knocked her over the Wall with your magic needle charm, and we captured her wand after you fell asleep," added Violet. "But she never likes to leave a job unfinished, so you should be careful about relaxing your guard too much."

"We must go," Sunny told her, a hint of sadness creeping into her voice at the thought. "Now that we've fulfilled our mission, we can only appear to you again during times of trouble. But be assured that we will always watch over you."

As the twelve fairies flitted out of the garden, they called back to her, "Farewell for now. Be safe!"

12

Dream Come True

The next day was Saturday, the day of the Grimmstone Library Games. However, before all the students could head to the library for the fun to begin, an announcement was piped through loudspeakers into every corner of Grimm Academy.

"This morning's event in the library has been canceled by Principal Wicked's order," chorused the School Board helmet-heads. "That is all."

"What? Why?" said Rose. She and Pea stood in their dorm room and looked at each other in disappointment.

"I'll tell you why," huffed Pea. "Because that lady is just plain mean. Not to mention evil."

Within minutes, all the girls began to gather on the walkways between the dorms, feeling rather glum. But soon Cinda suggested that they hold at least some of the events in the dorm towers on their own, instead of in the library. A scavenger hunt began and spirits rose. Ms. Wicked couldn't keep them down!

As Rose was searching for a shoe buckle — one of the items on the scavenger hunt list — she came upon Red sitting on a bench reading her handbook. "I'm looking for a new play," Red explained. "The last one the GA drama department performed was called *Red Robin Hood*. It was a success, but now we need something new. Something with a big cast, so more students can have parts in it and get some experience at acting."

"How about *A Midsummer Night's Dream*?" suggested Rose. "It's by a writer named William Shakespeare." She began to describe the plot and how there were bunches of fairies in it. "I even know some actual fairies who might be able to give the actors some tips," Rose told Red.

"Grimmawesome idea!" Red enthused. She sat up straighter as her interest keened.

Eagerly, she spoke to her handbook, requesting to view the play. When it appeared, she began to read, seeming to forget that Rose was there. But when Rose started to leave, Red looked up and said, "Think you could help us make the sets? And maybe do some acting if we put this play on? That needle of yours will come in really handy for stitching scenery backdrops. And for sword-fighting scenes. I mean, if you're staying on at GA?" Red asked hopefully.

Would she stay? She didn't have to, Rose realized. Not anymore. Despite the fairies' parting warnings, she didn't really think the curse remained a huge danger to herself or anyone else. So her parents would probably let her return home.

Before she could reply, she heard a familiar rhythmic thumping sound. Looking from the tower walkway down to the ground below, she saw her unicorn galloping toward the Academy.

"Starlight!" she cried out, overjoyed to see him. Bidding Red a hasty farewell, Rose raced downstairs, outside, and across the Academy's lawn. When she met her unicorn, she wrapped both arms around his snowy-white neck, hugging him. He tossed his head and nuzzled her, happy to see her, too.

"Where? How?" she began. But then she noticed a card attached to his horn with a ribbon. After untying the ribbon, she opened the card. It was from her parents. Sending Starlight to GA was her birthday present from them. And they apparently weren't far behind the unicorn, because the card said they were coming to visit her in their coach today. They'd only just heard what had happened yesterday and wanted to see for themselves that she was safe.

Rose leaped onto Starlight's back. "Come on, boy! Let's

go meet them." She planned to tell them she wanted to remain at the Academy, a decision she'd made on the spot right then and there. She'd tell Red and Pea, and her other new friends when she returned. And on Monday, she'd switch to Drama class instead of Comportment, so she and her needle could help Red with the new play.

Not only that, she would ask her parents' permission to officially begin knight training at the Academy. There was trouble brewing here. E.V.I.L. trouble. And she was determined to stay and fight. For in her heart she'd sworn to protect Grimm Academy and all of Grimmlandia. And she was going to uphold that promise!

"One day, when I'm a real knight, we'll ride to the Wall," she told her unicorn as they cantered across the lawn. "We'll see what's on the other side. And fight it until E.V.I.L. loses its power." And maybe someday, the curse upon Grimmlandia, for that's what the Society was in her opinion, would be destroyed once and for all.

Spying the coach ahead, she urged Starlight into a gallop. Together, they fairly flew across the fields to greet her parents, who loved her and cared about her. It was a magical moment. The wind was in her hair. She could smell the trees and flowers. The sky was sunny and blue. And the Academy lay behind her, awaiting her return.

When she had first arrived at GA, she never imagined she'd make such good friends, foil her fairy tale curse, have a chance to become a knight, and even meet a maybe-crush who wanted to be a writer. Not to mention save herself from a life of boredom and a Hundred Year Nap!

It was all like a dream come true!

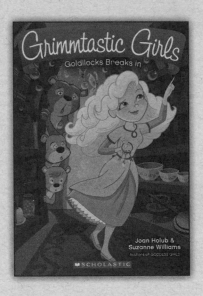

Goldilocks is so eager to make friends at Grimm Academy, she's even tempted to accept an invitation to join E.V.I.L. — it's just nice to be included! But she doesn't want to be a villain. Can Goldie get inside the secret society and do some good?

From the authors of
Goddess Girls–your
Grimmtastic
fairy-tale adventure awaits!

Read the whole Grimmtastic series!

Each time Abby and Jonah get sucked into their magic mirror, they wind up in a different fairy tale — and find new adventures!

Read all the
Whatever After books!

www.scholastic.com/whateverafter